凱信企管

用對的方法充實自己，
讓人生變得更美好！

凱信企管

用對的方法充實自己，
讓人生變得更美好！

凱信企管

用對的方法充實自己，
讓人生變得更美好！

凱信企管

用對的方法充實自己，
讓人生變得更美好！

English Reading

英文閱讀

高分特訓

克漏字＋解題攻略，
閱讀力及成績倍速飆升

PRFACE
作者序

　　你對英文閱讀總是心生恐懼嗎？

　　每一次大考閱讀測驗，答案總是用猜的嗎？……

　　或許你正點頭如搗蒜。

　　但偏偏閱讀測驗是許多重要大考的必考項目，為了拿高分，你，千萬不能放棄啊！

　　其實想要拿下閱讀測驗的高分，除了增加自身的詞彙庫以及高頻率的閱讀習慣之外，藉由「寫練習題」的方式，也是很好的鍛鍊方式。

　　所謂「熟能生巧」，這就是本書提供最大的目的。讓你藉由平時不斷地做練習來熟悉不同的題型，同時將所學在試題裡反覆的複習使其內化，英文能力勢必大大提升。

　　平常做英文閱讀測驗題目時，你是逐字逐句地閱讀文章還是你知道更有效率的閱讀方式？

　　如何快速抓到文章重點？先看文章還是先看題目？

　　到底怎麼做才能夠精準、快速的做答及得分呢？

　　本書針對不同題型提供有效的解題技巧，重要的測驗題及文章中譯、解析，說明更是淺顯易懂、一讀就理解，除了能助深度學習，也協助在做完練習後，確實訂正，方便您吸收解題技巧和文法重點，絕對是您平時增強閱讀測驗最佳的鍛鍊選擇。

　　多元主題、多樣知識，寫測驗鍛鍊之餘，還提供充實的閱讀體驗，如能一步一腳印善用本書，詳讀每一篇內文及寫練習題，相信英文實力與應考技巧一定能夠突飛猛進，即使面對大考也能信心十足。

CONTENTS
目 錄

Part II

測驗題鍛鍊

Chapter

1 單句填空題

解題技巧

此單元必須完全理解單字及前後文意來選擇答案，亦可利用文法的提示來刪除不正確的干擾字。因此，本單元要特別小心拼字相似、字義相似的單字，或單字的詞性變化，以免被混淆或誤導喔！

___ 1. If there _____ procrastination or any change of the conference, please contact me at your earliest possible convenience.

(A) will be
(B) should be
(C) is
(D) was

___ 2. _____ is our latest catalogue of skin care products. If you need some more information or test samples, please let us know.

(A) Enclosed
(B) Provided
(C) Inserted
(D) Supplied

___ 3. We would appreciate any feedback so that we can develop better products to _____ the customers' need.

(A) ignore
(B) tally
(C) meet
(D) conform

___ 4. We highly value the partnership with you over the years, and hope to continuously _____ you _____ the best service.

(A) provide; with
(B) aid; with
(C) thank; for
(D) protect; from

___ 5. It is sad to learn that Mr. Brook got _____ together with hundreds of other workers when the company downsized.

(A) promoted
(B) raised
(C) laid off
(D) exiled

___ 6. With all due respect, there must be some problem with the company if its employee _____ is high.

(A) loyalty
(B) welfare
(C) turnover
(D) counseling

___ 7. We need to _____ your performance before we give you a raise.

(A) evaluate
(B) calculate
(C) abandon
(D) deliberate

❶ 單句填空題

___ 8. Mr. Laurence, may I remind you that there will be a
_____ charge if you want to change your order.

(A) cancellation
(B) handling
(C) admission
(D) registration

___ 9. Since the team members were all carefully
selected from each department in our company,
I'm sure they will _____ our expectations and
accomplish the task.

(A) get the better of
(B) live up to
(C) go against
(D) take root in

___ 10. The rumor about our Finance Manager's
defalcation has already _____ through the
office.

(A) advertised
(B) circulated
(C) infected
(D) intruded

___ 11. Our company has connections with many firms in Europe and the U.S. Therefore all employees are _____ to speak English and French fluently.

(A) required
(B) examined
(C) prejudiced
(D) voluntary

___ 12. All staff please _____ in the conference room at ten o'clock. We're going to have an emergency meeting.

(A) centralize
(B) concentrate
(C) accumulate
(D) assemble

___ 13. It is said that the workers are forming a combination to _____ their rights and interests.

(A) stand against
(B) set foot on
(C) fight for
(D) compete against

___ 14. Excellent _____ between supervisors and subordinates is essential to a happy working environment.

(A) communication
(B) confrontation
(C) agreement
(D) interference

___ 15. Lower labor cost gives China a comparative advantage at _____ manufactures.

(A) purchasing
(B) importing
(C) producing
(D) contacting

___ 16. In order to _____ their products, we need to lower the market prices of our commodities.

(A) cross out
(B) turn down
(C) draw back
(D) compete with

___ 17. The two companies announced their cooperation program in the press _____.

(A) appointment
(B) conference
(C) interview
(D) meeting

___ 18. After seeing John's presentation, we have to
_____ that he is very adequate to this job.

(A) decide

(B) apply

(C) prevail

(D) acknowledge

___ 19. Tony was fired for leaking out the _____
document of the company.

(A) confident

(B) complimentary

(C) confidential

(D) classical

___ 20. To _____ the meeting to thirty minutes, we
need to focus our discussion on the main issue.

(A) prevent

(B) close

(C) control

(D) confine

___ 21. You might get fired if you don't conform to the
leave _____.

(A) provisions

(B) conditions

(C) situation

(D) legislation

❶
單
句
填
空
題

___ 22. The failure of this project was _____ on the irretrievable error he committed.

(A) consequent
(B) result
(C) outcome
(D) effect

___ 23. Congratulations! Your proposal to advertise the product is _____ .

(A) adapted
(B) eliminated
(C) adopted
(D) cancelled

___ 24. Rumor has it that the two companies will _____ and form a single large organization.

(A) merge
(B) separate
(C) connect
(D) disperse

___ 25. To achieve the result that we expect, there are still many problems to _____ with.

(A) content
(B) contend
(C) contest
(D) context

___ 26. According to this report, the prices of agricultural products have been increasing due to the _____ drought.

(A) potential
(B) regular
(C) continual
(D) historical

___ 27. We have received the bread machine that we ordered from your company, but I _____ to tell you that the quality of the machine is quite unsatisfactory.

(A) love
(B) regret
(C) suppose
(D) seldom

___ 28. Mr. White has _____ with Mike In the meeting room for hours.

(A) conversed
(B) conserved
(C) convened
(D) convinced

____ 29. The workers were very _____ that they worked overtime to get the project done in time.

(A) agreeable
(B) mutual
(C) cooperative
(D) self-absorbed

____ 30. It is heard that the company will _____ fifty hundred thousand dollars for updating the computer equipment in the office.

(A) boycott
(B) budget
(C) balance
(D) propose

____ 31. As a supervisor, you should treat your subordinates fairly without _____.

(A) limitation
(B) objection
(C) discrimination
(D) sentiments

____ 32. We'll throw a _____ party for a senior colleague who's going to retire next month.

(A) housewarming
(B) welcoming
(C) reunion
(D) farewell

___ 33. The interpreter's faulty interpretation _____ a
　　　 great misunderstanding between the two parties.

　　　 (A) straightened out
　　　 (B) cut down
　　　 (C) brought about
　　　 (D) come around

___ 34. You need to overcome the language barrier
　　　 _____ work for an international company.

　　　 (A) in order to
　　　 (B) as long as
　　　 (C) get over with
　　　 (D) so much as

___ 35. Few people in the office know that Mr. Bruce is
　　　 going to spend his _____ vacation in Maldives.

　　　 (A) maternal
　　　 (B) annual
　　　 (C) daily
　　　 (D) social

___ 36. The vacation leave policy is quite elastic in our
　　　 company. That means you can arrange your
　　　 holidays more _____.

　　　 (A) flexibly
　　　 (B) carefully
　　　 (C) attentively
　　　 (D) irrationally

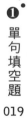

❶
單
句
填
空
題

___ 37. According to our personnel regulations, there will be a three-month probation period before you become a _____ employer.

(A) normal
(B) regular
(C) usual
(D) ordinary

___ 38. This letter is to inform you that Mr. Burton will hold the _____ while our General Manager is on a business trip.

(A) fort
(B) field
(C) ground
(D) breath

___ 39. Don't worry. The meat you ordered will be kept in a cooler in our truck during the _____.

(A) translation
(B) transmission
(C) transportation
(D) consignation

___ 40. All of the interviewers agreed that Ms. Cliff _____ all the qualifications for a flight attendant.

(A) fulfilled
(B) accompanied
(C) competent
(D) required

___ 41. Sally rarely has a day off after she got promoted to the General Manager. I hope she won't _____ herself from overwork.

(A) excite
(B) confuse
(C) exhaust
(D) bore

___ 42. _____ to the survey, 90% of the customers stay in business with us because of the outstanding customer service from our sales team.

(A) Regarding
(B) So as
(C) Owing
(D) According

___ 43. With all due respect, I really think you should set a more realistic goal which you can sensibly expect to _____ .

(A) kick
(B) achieve
(C) finish
(D) come

___ 44. I _____ know Mr. Smith was one of our shareholders until my boss introduced him to me.

(A) didn't
(B) shouldn't
(C) mustn't
(D) haven't

___ 45. Would you please have your assistant get all the promotional material ready and send a copy for our _____ by tomorrow?

(A) conference
(B) reference
(C) difference
(D) preference

___ 46. The employees _____ having to work on the weekends just as expected.

(A) rebelled at
(B) refused to
(C) reluctant to
(D) complained

___ 47. The factory had to _____ all the products that contained illegal ingredients within a week.

(A) cancel
(B) recall
(C) retrain
(D) detain

___ 48. Excuse me. Could you give me an _____ for my payment so that I can apply for the company expense?

(A) invoice
(B) approval
(C) agreement
(D) application

___ 49. The planning department arranged a spectacular _____ last weekend in order to welcome our new General Manager to our company.

(A) presentation
(B) debriefing
(C) reception
(D) seminar

___ 50. This is really not a good time to resign your current job, because it is very difficult to find jobs during the _____ .

(A) recession
(B) stress
(C) probation
(D) distraction

___ 51. As a competent operator, it is necessary to
memorize everyone's _____ number in the
office.

(A) registration
(B) extension
(C) stock
(D) serial

___ 52. The first thing Mr. Lewis did after _____ the
company was to reorganize it thoroughly.

(A) taking over
(B) putting upon
(C) crediting with
(D) pulling back

___ 53. Any ideas _____ at the meeting will be kept in
the minutes.

(A) bring up
(B) bringing up
(C) brought up
(D) are brought up

___ 54. According to the stipulation, you have to _____
for our loss.

(A) compensate
(B) consume
(C) encounter
(D) identify

___ 55. You will be _____ a three-month trial before you become regular employees.

(A) giving
(B) given
(C) gave
(D) give

___ 56. Jeff seems to _____ on his work lately. As a supervisor, you should remind him of his own duty.

(A) slack off
(B) keep up
(C) put his shirt on
(D) take stock

___ 57. His supervisor made quite _____ remarks on his performance. That's why he didn't get a raise this year.

(A) irregular
(B) negative
(C) pessimistic
(D) direct

___ 58. In case you forget, may I _____ you that our meeting begins at three this afternoon?

(A) notify
(B) inform
(C) remind
(D) warn

___ 59. Julia is going to substitute for Amy while she is
_____ bereavement leave.

(A) on
(B) for
(C) in
(D) under

___ 60. I quit, but I will still come to the office _____
they find a replacement.

(A) despite
(B) until
(C) as long as
(D) therefore

___ 61. The team spent several weeks _____ for the
presentation of their new proposal.

(A) to prepare
(B) preparing
(C) prepared
(D) prepare

___ 62. The customer returned the defective item and
demanded a _____ .

(A) reward
(B) review
(C) refund
(D) report

___ 63. You can send us an email and I will pass the information to related departments. They will contact you _____ it is necessary.

(A) whether
(B) if
(C) although
(D) unless

___ 64. The director _____ an unscheduled meeting of all the staff in his department.

(A) convened
(B) opened
(C) assembled
(D) gathered

___ 65. It was the unfair treatment from the company that _____ his resignation.

(A) came to
(B) led to
(C) brought in
(D) resulted from

___ 66. The customer _____ that we should compensate for his loss.

(A) insisted
(B) consisted
(C) resisted
(D) assisted

❶
單
句
填
空
題

___ 67. Employees' fierce opposition to the new regulation
is _____ .
(A) untrustful
(B) expectable
(C) contractual
(D) disposable

___ 68. I wrote a letter to your customer center to
complain about the product two weeks ago, but
haven't got any _____ so far.
(A) echo
(B) actions
(C) answers
(D) feedback

___ 69. Any business firms that want to participate in this
year's International Communication Trade Show
please be noted that the _____ for application
is September 15.
(A) duration
(B) period
(C) deadline
(D) length

___ 70. The spokesman of the labor union claimed that all workers should get reasonable pay _____ their hard work.

(A) in the light of
(B) in reward for
(C) for want of
(D) regardless of

___ 71. The _____ was so nervous that his voice was shaky when responding to the interviewer's questions.

(A) applicant
(B) supplier
(C) supervisor
(D) subordinate

___ 72. Rumor has it that the Director of the Sales Department will _____ to CBU Company, and it has spread across the office.

(A) retire
(B) job-hop
(C) resign
(D) lay off

___ 73. Generally, the selling prices of our products are
     20% _____ than their list prices.
     (A) lower
     (B) smaller
     (C) shorter
     (D) littler

___ 74. Thanks to Sales Department's marketing
     _____, the new product successfully gained
     publicity through giving out free samples.
     (A) trick
     (B) strategy
     (C) access
     (D) practice

___ 75. I'm sorry, but no one can enter the generator
     room without _____ .
     (A) order
     (B) permission
     (C) attention
     (D) allowance

___ 76. According to the train's timetable, the next train
     _____ Taipei will be leaving at 3:06 p.m.
     (A) bound for
     (B) drive in
     (C) go after
     (D) attend to

___ 77. That the engineer's death from _____ revealed the fact that many companies are forcing their employees to work overtime.

(A) earthquake
(B) overwork
(C) cancer
(D) depression

___ 78. The contract needs both parties' signatures to be

_____ .

(A) efficient
(B) infectious
(C) effective
(D) affective

___ 79. I'm sorry, but our CEO is not _____ now and I'm afraid that I can't pass the CEO's contact information to you.

(A) available
(B) attachable
(C) acceptable
(D) acquirable

___ 80. We don't have specific dress code in the office, but I'm sure miniskirts and hot pants are not _____ for work.

(A) appropriate

(B) equitable

(C) enough

(D) adapted

（答案＆解析，詳見P136）

Chapter

2 短文閱讀
克漏字

文內容大多以書信及敘述文為主，只須根據內文的提示，並觀察前後文，即可做出正確選擇。

重點提示：必須閱讀超過一個句子才能找到答案。

📝 短文閱讀 1

Dear Mr. Breaux,

I am writing to inform you that I won't be able to meet with you on Thursday as _____ . The company has a

1. (A) scheduled
   (B) ordered
   (C) approval
   (D) commitment

marketing event from Tuesday till the weekend, and I was _____as the person in charge. So I will be out of

2. (A) asked
   (B) nominated
   (C) permitted
   (D) given

town for the following week. I understand that you may need another sales person to help you with your business without delay, so I suggest you _____

3. (A) contacted
   (B) contacting
   (C) be contacted
   (D) contact

Ryan Blinn, our regional manager. He will _____ you _____ with another sales person.

4. (A) make; up
   (B) set; up
   (C) look;on
   (D) end; up

His email address is ryanblinn_south@tbc.com.tw and his contact number is 0988123456.

Please accept my sincere _____ for not being

5. (A) apologize
   (B) apology
   (C) sorry
   (D) regretful

able to provide you with my service this time. Hopefully I will have the chance to help you with your business in the near future.

Sincerely yours,
Tammy Huang

（答案＆解析，詳見P162）

📝 短文閱讀 2

To: Mr. Samuel Wang
From: C.N.B. Return Processing Center
Subject: Your Request of Returning a DOA Product

Dear Mr. Wang,

We have received your request of returning a dead on arrival product.

Before we _____ the action, we need to inform

1. (A) proceed with
   (B) deal with
   (C) keep up
   (D) hold back

you that you can ask foreither a replacement for the _____ product or a refund for this sale.

2. (A) fragile
   (B) specified
   (C) defective
   (D) ineffective

If you need a _____ , we will send you a new

3. (A) debt
   (B) environment
   (C) receipt
   (D) replacement

item and of course we will be responsible for the shipping cost. If you prefer a refund, please provide us the original purchase _____ and the shipping slip.

4. (A) proof
   (B) witness
   (C) evidence
   (D) receipt

Please be noted that we will need you to send the faulty item back to us along with related documents either way you choose.

We sincerely apologize for the inconvenience.

_____ you have any questions, please feel free to

5. (A) Although
   (B) Perhaps
   (C) Must
   (D) Should

contact us.

（答案＆解析，詳見P164）

📝 短文閱讀 3

Good morning, ladies and gentlemen. This is your captain speaking. Welcome on South East Airline Flight 168. We are currently cruising at an _____ of

1. (A) attitude
   (B) altitude
   (C) substitute
   (D) latitude

430,000 feet at a speed of 400 miles per hour. The time is 8: 15 a.m. The _____ in Tokyo is clear and sunny.

2. (A) temperature
   (B) weather
   (C) scenery
   (D) entertainment

We are _____ to land in Narita Airport approximately

3. (A) believing
   (B) deciding
   (C) expecting
   (D) finding

ten minutes ahead of schedule. The cabin _____ will

4. (A) employees
   (B) workers
   (C) crew
   (D) ladies

be coming around in about fifteen minutes to _____

5. (A) offer
   (B) hand
   (C) show
   (D) supply

you beverages. Please sit back, relax and enjoy the rest of the flight.

（答案＆解析，詳見P166）

If you travel, you need a credit card with the flexibility to match. The CTB Premier Credit Card, a local card with a world of benefits, _____ at over

1. (A) will accept
   (B) is accepted
   (C) is accepting
   (D) accepted

15,000 locations worldwide, and the _____ include:

2. (A) comments
   (B) compilers
   (C) advantages
   (D) investments

- A local best in class rewards programme that _____ you to superb offers

3. (A) entitles
   (B) enables
   (C) allows
   (D) permits

on shopping, dining, entertaining and travel experiences around the world.

・ Emergency cash advance of US $2,000 and next-day card replacement in the event of _____ or loss.

4. (A) thief
   (B) stolen
   (C) theft
   (D) stealing

・ A _____ credit card for you or your child with full emergency assistance

5. (A) attachment
   (B) added
   (C) supplementary
   (D) accessory

and support plus a credit limit that you control.

（答案＆解析，詳見P168）

📝 短文閱讀 5

Ladies and gentlemen, welcome onboard Flight EI385 with service from Shanghai to London. We are currently in the third runway for take-off and are expected to be _____ in approximately five minutes.

1. (A) in the air
   (B) in-flight
   (C) on-air
   (D) uploaded

We _____ that you please fasten your seatbelts and

2. (A) suppose
   (B) assure
   (C) request
   (D) apply

secure all baggage underneath your seat or in the overhead cabinets. We also need you to make sure _____ your seats and tray tables are in the upright

3. (A) for
   (B) where
   (C) which
   (D) that

position for take-off. Please turn off all personal electronic _____ , including laptops and cell phones.

4. (A) supplies
   (B) devices
   (C) implements
   (D) machinery

Smoking is _____ for the duration of the flight. Thank you for your

5. (A) limited
   (B) controlled
   (C) prohibited
   (D) avoidable

cooperation. Asia-East Airlines wish you a pleasant journey.

（答案＆解析，詳見P170）

❷
短文閱讀克漏字

U-Tech Electronics Ltd Taipei

August 15, 2010

Robert Dean
No. 308, XinYi Road, XinYi district, Taipei
Tel: 56042209#55
Fax: 56042200
e-mail: robertdean@utech.org.tw
website: www.u-tech.sh.org.tw

To Nelson Jones,
    We regret to inform you that you are _____
contract as regards the agreement

1. (A) in the control of
   (B) in breach of
   (C) under the flag of
   (D) in behalf of

you signed with us dated 10 April in 2009. Therein you
had clearly committed yourself _____ secrecy of the

2. (A) maintaining
   (B) to maintain
   (C) to maintaining
   (D) that maintaining

details with reference to any of the technical aspects of the new smart touch mobile phone until after the _____. The speech

3. (A) launch
   (B) disclosure
   (C) revelation
   (D) marketing

you gave last week not only violates the contract, _____

4. (A) but
   (B) or
   (C) also
   (D) and

contains negative comments that may harm the release of our product. Please be noted that we will have no choice but to take legal action unless a formal and public retraction _____

5. (A) will be made
   (B) made
   (C) has been made
   (D) is made

by the end of August, 2010.

Sincerely,
Robert Dean

（答案＆解析，詳見172）

❷
短文閱讀克漏字

Chapter

3 長文閱讀測驗

解題技巧

長篇文章，更能培養閱讀及解題的耐性。
閱讀文章前先將問題讀一遍，再掃描整
篇內容，即能較快的找到答案。遇到雙
篇文章時，須特別注意比對兩篇文章的關連性，以免造成選擇
失誤。

📝 長文閱讀 1

Customer Support Analyst (Contract)

Responsibilities

★ provide technical assistance to users through phone, emails or fax.

★ provide 1st and 2nd level support and troubleshooting.

★ log problem onto Service Desk database.

★ provide end-to-end problem management.

★ ensure continuous improvement to the job function.

★ submit daily, weekly and monthly helpdesk report to team leader.

★ manage the helpdesk database.

Requirements

★ candidates must possesses at least a diploma or degree in Computer Science equivalent.

★ 1-2 year(s) of working experience in related field.

★ required skill(s): Microsoft Window OS, Basic Networking, Window XP, Microsoft Outlook 2011 and Remote Access troubleshooting.

★ able to speak English, Japanese and Chinese.

★ possesses good communication and interpersonal skills.

★ applicants will be based in Tokyo, Japan.

★ applicants should be R.O.C. citizens.

___ 1. What is the purpose of this advertisement?

(A) To encourage employees to take computer courses.

(B) To ask employees to take their own responsibilities.

(C) To recruit a contracted customer support analyst.

(D) To ask their employees to improve their customer service.

___ 2. According to the advertisement, the applicants for this position should be?

(A) trilingual.

(B) a Japanese.

(C) under 35 years old.

(D) able to work immediately.

___ 3. Which of the following is excluded from the responsibilities of the customer support analyst?

(A) To provide technical assistance to users.

(B) To submit daily report to team leader.

(C) To possess good interpersonal skills.

(D) To manage the helpdesk database.

___ 4. According to the advertisement, what does the word candidates mean?

(A) Suspects.

(B) Employers.

(C) Professors.

(D) Applicants.

___ 5. According to the advertisement, which statement is NOT TRUE?

(A) One of the responsibilities is providing technical assistance to users through emails.

(B) Working experience in related field is not necessary.

(C) You have to possesse good communication and interpersonal skills If you want to get the job.

(D) Candidates must possesses at least a diploma or degree in Computer Science equivalent.

（答案＆解析，詳見P175）

Transfer/ Transit Procedures

If you are taking a connecting flight at Hong Kong International Airport, please pay attention to the steps listed below.

For passengers with an onward boarding pass, please:

★ Follow the directional sign to departure level for boarding gates.

★ Go through security check.

★ Check your gate number and time, and reach your boarding gate at least 30 minutes before departure time.

For passengers without an onward boarding pass, please:

★ Check your airline desk's location.

★ Follow the directional sign to the designated Airline Desk Areas E1, E2 or W1 for check-in;

★ Follow the directional sign to departure level for boarding gates.

★ Go through security check.

★ Check your gate number and time, and reach your boarding gate at least 30 minutes before departure time.

___ 1. Where is this notice most likely to be seen?

(A) In an exotic restaurant.

(B) At the airport.

(C) At the check-in counter of a hotel.

(D) At a tourist agency.

___ 2. According to the notice, when should the passengers reach their boarding gates at the latest?

(A) Two hours before the take-off time.

(B) An hour after the flight arrived.

(C) Half an hour before the arrival time.

(D) Half an hour before the take-off time.

___ 3. According to the notice, what do passengers without an onward boarding pass do before going to the departure level for boarding gates?

(A) Check in at the airline desk.

(B) Claim their baggage.

(C) Ask the flight attendants for a new boarding pass.

(D) Call their tourist agency for help.

___ 4. According to the notice, which of the following is NOT mentioned?

(A) Baggage weight allowance.
(B) Follow the directional sign to departure level for boarding gates.
(C) Follow the directional sign to the designated Airline Desk Areas E1, E2 or W1 for check-in if a passenger doesn't have an onward boarding pass.
(D)The boading time.

___ 5. According to the notice, what does the word procedure refer to?

(A) Incident.
(B) Process.
(C) Program.
(D) Development.

（答案＆解析，詳見P178）

Bonus Days Off 2023/12/22 and 2023/12/29

October 29, 2023

Dear Staff Colleagues:

I know that many of you are now beginning to make plans for the winter holidays. We all look forward to time with family and friends after a busy fall semester. While hard work is the foundation of TBS's excellence, we all need to balance work with time off for renewal.

Accordingly, I am pleased to announce that this year the company will give all staff both Friday, December 23, 2023, and Friday, December 22, 2023, as bonus days off, in addition to the previously announced holidays on December 24 and 25 and January 1. These bonus days will apply to all benefits-eligible TBS staff. The provision of necessary services will require some staff to work on December 22 and December 29. Supervisors will be in touch with those of you who need to come in those days, and will determine whether you can identify two other days to take as bonus days or will receive comparable pay. I appreciate your flexibility and understanding.

I hope that these extra days off will make the upcoming holidays just a little bit more pleasant for each of you.

Best regards,

Maggie

Margarita S. Cliff

Personnel Manager

___ 1. What messages is this announcement trying to pass to the colleagues?

(A) The company is going to lay off half of the staff.

(B) The company is giving all staff bonus days off.

(C) The company will be merged with TBS.

(D) The company requires all staff to work on Christmas.

___ 2. According to the announcement, what is the option that the staff who has to work on December 23 or 30 may have?

(A) To receive comparable pay.

(B) To find others to hold the fort for them.

(C) To ask for sick leave.

(D) To complain to the labor union.

___ 3. In the second paragraph, who of the following may be excluded from the "benefits-eligible" staff?

(A) The regular staff of TBS.

(B) The personnel manager, Maggie.

(C) The day labor.

(D) The office assistant.

___ 4. How would the staff feel after reading the announcement?

(A)They would feel frustrated.

(B)They would feel worried.

(C)They would feel terrible.

(D)They would feel happy.

___ 5. According to the announcement, which statement is TRUE ?

(A) The announcement is announced after December 25.

(B) The TBS Company will give all staff three more holidays.

(C) Maggie announces the announcement.

(D) The supervisors will have to work on December 29.

（答案＆解析，詳見P181）

❸

長
文
閱
讀
測
驗

U.S. jobless drops to 8.8%, two-year low

WASHINGTON -- The unemployment rate in the United States was last reported at a two-year low of 8.8 percent in March of 2011. From 1948 until 2010 the United States' Unemployment Rate averaged 5.70 percent reaching an historical high of 10.80 percent in November of 1982 and a record low of 2.50 percent in May of 1953.

"They are very consistent with the view that the recovery is gaining some momentum. So the economy continues to recover, it's very good news," said Hugh Johnson, chief investment officer at Hugh Johnson Advisors in Albany, New York.

U.S. Non-farm payroll employment increased by 216,000 in March. Job gains occurred in professional and business services, health care, leisure and hospitality, and mining. Employment in manufacturing continued to trend up.

The private sector accounted for all the new jobs in March, adding 230,000 positions after February's 240,000 increase. Government employment fell 14,000, declining for a fifth straight month as local governments let go 15,000 workers.

Although rising energy prices are eroding consumer confidence, economists do not expect businesses to put the brakes on hiring just yet.

"Employment gains have been modest in recent months, so in that sense I think businesses that were initially very wary of taking on permanent full-time employees are feeling more confident now than some months ago," said Richard DeKaser, an economist at Parthenon Group in Boston. "As a result they are more willing to make those kinds of long-term commitments."

___ 1. What can we learn from this news?
   (A) The U.S. is undergoing the economy recession.
   (B) Consumer confidence boosts as a result of the rising energy prices.
   (C) The public sector added 14,000 positions in March of 2011.
   (D) It seems that the economy in the U.S. is recovering.

___ 2. According to the news, which of the following is true?

   (A) U.S. local governments laid off 15,000 workers in the past five months.
   (B) Businesses are still cautious about taking on long-term fulltime employees.
   (C) Employment in all trades and professions increased except manufacturing.
   (D) Businesses are more confident of hiring temporary workers than permanent ones.

___ 3. According to the news, which of the following results in erosion of consumer confidence?

   (A) That more businesses are willing to make long-term commitments to employees.
   (B) That government employment has been declining for a fifth straight month.
   (C) That energy prices continue to rise regardless of the recovering economy.
   (D) That businesses are expected to put the brakes on hiring full-time employees.

___ 4. According to the news, what does the phrase "trend up" in paragraph 3 refer to?

   (A) Decrease.
   (B) Rise.
   (C) Allow.
   (D) Modify.

___ 5. According to the news, why businesses are more willing to make those kinds of long-term commitments?

(A) Because they don't need to hire more employees.

(B) Because they will make more money in the future.

(C) Because businesses that were initially wary of taking on permanent full-time employees are feeling more confident now than some months ago.

(D) Because economists gave them some good advice.

（答案＆解析，詳見P184）

Dear Ms. Jennifer Bao,

It was a pleasure to meet with you last Friday, March 31, 2023.

We were very impressed with your outstanding book-editing background and your years at Caves Books. After discussing your application with our General Editor, I am delighted to offer you the position of editor-in-chief, with the salary of NT$42,000 per month. As for the benefits, you will receive National Health Insurance for you as well as labor insurance. More details will be discussed if you are interested in accepting the position.

Please give your serious consideration to this job offer and send me an acknowledgement by the end of this Friday, April 8.

We sincerely look forward to welcoming you to our team.

Best regards,

Andy Hsiao
Manager of Human Resource Division

___ 1. What can we learn about Jennifer Bao from this letter?

    (A) She has no related working experience in book-editing.

    (B) She just graduated from college this year.

    (C) She had a job interview last week.

    (D) She decided not to accept the job offer.

___ 2. Which job position was Jennifer Bao most likely to apply for?

    (A) The general editor.

    (B) The editor-in-chief.

    (C) The assistant editor.

    (D) The manager of human resource division.

___ 3. When should Jennifer Bao reply this letter at the latest?

    (A) March 31, 2023.

    (B) April 8, 2023.

    (C) The end of April.

    (D) The end of 2023.

___ 4. What is the purpose of this letter?

(A) To make a formal complaint at work.

(B) To make a job offer to a candidate.

(C) To require to complete the job before April 8.

(D) To announce salary increase.

___ 5. What does the word "outstanding" is closest in meaning to?

(A) Complex.

(B) Horrible.

(C) Interesting.

(D) Remarkable.

（答案＆解析，詳見P187）

📝 **長文閱讀 6**

Shelton ® *Car Rental*

Name: ***Chang Bo En***
Passport No. ***P1269573400***

Renting City, Airport Code or US Zip code of the location
Lancaster Airport
☑ I'm returning this rental car to a different Shelton car rental location.

Returning City, Airport Code or US Zip code of the location
Allentown L V I Airport

Pick Up Date and Time:
13/04/2023-10:00

Return Date and Time:
03/05/2023-14:00

Rental Car Type:
Fullsize/Standard:
These vehicles generally have 4 doors, seat 4 to 5 passengers, and have luggage capacity of up to 4 to 5 suitcases (luggage capacity varies by luggage size and vehicle model).

☐ I have a discount (CDP, PC, Coupon or other code)

___ 1. What is the main purpose of this form?

    (A) To make a reservation for a rental car.

    (B) To cancel a reservation for a restaurant.

    (C) To confirm a reservation for a flight ticket.

    (D) To make an appointment with the dentist.

___ 2. What can we learn about Chang Bo En from this form?

    (A) He will be at the Allentown LVI Airport on April 13, 2023.

    (B) He wants to rent an apartment in Lancaster.

    (C) He will return the car at the same place where he picks it up.

    (D) He has to rent the car without a discount.

___ 3. How long will Chang Bo En need the car?

    (A) For about three weeks.

    (B) For nearly a week.

    (C) For four hours.

    (D) Not mentioned.

___ 4. Where will Chang Bo En return the car?

    (A) Allentown L V I Airport.

    (B) Sydney.

    (C) New York Ariport.

    (D) Lancaster Airport

___ 5. According to this form, which statement is TRUE?

(A) The rental car type is truck.

(B) Chang Bo En will return the vehicle on April 13th.

(C) Chang Bo En uses his passport to rent the car.

(D) The vehicle has 2 doors and has luggage capacity of up to two suitcases.

（答案＆解析，詳見P189）

📝 長文閱讀 7

Removal Notice

To our valued Customers and Partners,

　Please be Informed that our office will be moved to the following address
with effective from 1st October 2010, which is located next to our old office.

　Room 1033-1035, 10/F., Prince Building,
　No. 223, Lane 288,
　Sec. 4, Zhong Xiao E. Rd.,
　Da An District, Taipei

Our telephone and fax numbers remain unchanged.

Yours sincerely,
Flyer Shipping Ltd.

___ 1. What is this notice mainly about?

   (A) A notification about the relocation of the office.

   (B) An announcement of business suspension.

   (C) An announcement of business reopening.

   (D) An advertisement for staff recruitment.

___ 2. According to the notice, when will the new office be effective?

   (A) Within the next few days.

   (B) This very day.

   (C) The beginning of October in 2010.

   (D) Some day in October of 2011.

___ 3. By which of the following ways will customers or partners fail in making contact with Flyer Shipping Ltd.?

   (A) By calling at Flyer Shipping's original number.

   (B) By faxing a letter at Flyer Shipping's original number.

   (C) By paying personal visit at the new location.

   (D) By sending mails to the original address.

___ 4. Which of the following is true about this notice?

   (A) The office will be moved to far away from here.

   (B) Their phone number remain unchanged.

   (C) The office will reopen in September.

   (D) There is no elevator in the Price Building.

___ 5. According to the notice, which of the following is NOT mentioned?

(A) The name of the company.

(B) The name of the owner.

(C) The reopening date.

(D)The fax number.

（答案＆解析，詳見P191）

📝 長文閱讀 8

The Council of Labor Affairs (CLA) announced the other day that an investigation had concluded that the sudden death of a 29-year-old man who regularly worked overtime at NY Technology Corp was caused by overwork.

The victim, Hsu, started working at NY in 2006 as an engineer and frequently worked overtime. Before his death, Hsu had been putting in about 80 hours of overtime each month for half a year, sometimes as much as 139 hours a month.

The case first came to the public's attention in September when Hsu's parents at a press conference claimed that Hsu had died of exhaustion. As he did not have any previous illnesses and was in the prime of his life, suddenly dying from heart attack or stroke were classic signs of death from overwork.

Council officials refused to recognize the case as death from overwork at first because they found that Hsu died of cardiogenic shock, which was unrelated to his occupation. Nevertheless, the council reassessed the case and said that Hsu's death should have been categorized as death from overwork because the second investigation showed that Hsu's sudden death was strongly correlated with his long-term working overtime.

Lawmakers and labor activists had long accused the council of turning a blind eye to hazardous work environments and the near impossibility of getting fair compensation for death from overwork under the current system.

The Bureau of Labor Insurance will be taking over this case, and is likely to compensate the worker's family the equivalent of 45 months' salary.

___ 1. According to the article, what was the cause of the 29-year-old engineer's death?

(A) A congenital heart disease.
(B) Drug overdose.
(C) Long-term working overtime.
(D) Alcohol intoxication.

___ 2. According to the article, what are classic signs of death from overwork?

(A) Sudden death from heart attack or stroke.

(B) Chronic melancholia or panic disorder.

(C) Chronic insomnia or weariness.

(D) Death from respiratory distress.

___ 3. According to the article, which of the statements is true?

(A) The victim's family is not likely to get any compensation for their son's death from overwork.

(B) The Bureau of Labor Insurance is likely to pay 45 months' salary in compensation for the death of the victim.

(C) CLA categorized the engineer's death as death from overwork as soon as the case came to the public's attention.

(D) Labor activists are satisfied with the efforts that CLA has made to improve the current work environments.

___ 4. According to the article, what is the word "occupation" in paragraph 4 closest in meaning to?

(A) Transportation.

(B) Job.

(C) Investment.

(D) Background.

❸
長
文
閱
讀
測
驗

___ 5. If the Bureau of Labor Insurance take over this case, how much may they compensate the worker's family?

(A) The equivalent of 12 months' salary.

(B) The equivalent of 45 months' salary.

(C) At least one hundred thousand dollars.

(D) It doesn't mention.

（答案＆解析，詳見P193）

March 15, 2011

Lost & Found Notice

The Office of General Affairs is holding items found in various locations throughout the office building. The items that have been recovered are as followed: keys, mobile phones, iPods, digital cameras, CDs, CD Player, earrings, money, wallets, watches and miscellaneous items.

If you have lost items such as these and can identify them accurately, call David Tang, Director of General Affairs Division @ extension 8308.

All items not claimed within 14 days, following the date of this listing, will be put up to auction or be donated to charities without further ado.

___ 1. According to the notice, when should the owners claim their lost items?

(A) No later than March 28, 2011.
(B) No later than March 15, 2011.
(C) No later than the end of the week.
(D) No later than the last day of March.

___ 2. According to the notice, where should the staff claim their lost items?

    (A) The police station.

    (B) The guardroom.

    (C) The office of General Affairs.

    (D) The reception room.

___ 3. According to the notice, how will the lost items not claimed be disposed of?

    (A) To be destroyed by burning.

    (B) To be sold at auction.

    (C) To be sold to charities.

    (D) To be discarded as rubbish.

___ 4. In the first paragraph, the word "miscellaneous" is closest in meaning to?

    (A) assorted.

    (B) classified.

    (C) collected

    (D) random.

___ 5. According to the notice, which statement is NOT TRUE ?

    (A) The Lost &Found Notice is posted in March.

    (B) If you have lost items, you can call Director of General Affairs Division @ extension 8308.

    (C) All items not claimed within 10 days.

    (D) The items that have been recovered include digital cameras.

（答案＆解析，詳見P196）

From: Mr. Daniel Watson,
Director of Daisy & Daniel's
To: Mr. Thomas Rodman
Date: 2011-04-12
Subject: Business Event Invitation

Dear Mr. Rodman,

I hope that this letter finds you in the best of health and spirit. As you are among our valued customer, we would like to thank you for your business and would take this opportunity to invite you for the launch of our new apparel series on 10th of May, 2011 at 5 p.m. at Hotel Regent.

An opening ceremony and then a dinner party are organized just to extend our gratitude to our guests. We want to introduce our new line of fashion apparel to our valued clients and customers, so we want all our guests to attend the party.

Please give us your confirmation by 30th of April, 2011.

Your presence is thus sought for.

Sincerely Yours,
Daniel Watson

From: Mr. Thomas Rodman
To: Mr. Daniel Watson,
Subject: Re: Business Event Invitation

Dear Daniel,

Thanks for your kind invitation. Unfortunately, due to a prior commitment on the date of your function, I regret that I will be unable to attend the opening ceremony.

Please accept my sincere congratulations on the launch of your new apparel series.
Hope we could arrange a time to get together after the celebration.

Yours,
Thomas Rodman

___ 1. What can we learn from the e-mails?

   (A) Mr. Rodman was invited to Mr. Watson's wedding ceremony.
   (B) Mr. Rodman declined the invitation because of a prior engagement.
   (C) There will be a press conference at Hotel Regent.
   (D) Mr. Rodman will attend the ceremony in person.

___ 2. On which of the following dates is the responding
e-mail most likely to be sent?

(A) 28th of April, 2011.
(B) 10th of May, 2011.
(C) 28th of May, 2011.
(D) 10th of April, 2011.

___ 3. According to the emails, what is the relation
between Mr. Rodman and Mr. Watson?

(A) They are employer and employee.
(B) They are old family friends.
(C) They are distant relatives.
(D) They have dealings in business.

___ 4. What kind of occasion is Mr. Rodman invited to?

(A) A new product launch.
(B) A year-end party.
(C) An academic seminar.
(D) An engagement ceremony.

_____ 5. Which of the following statements cannot be inferred from the e-mails?

(A) Thomas Rodman has an engagement on the same date that Daisy & Daniel's is going to launch their new apparel series.

(B) Thomas Rodman hopes he and Mr. Watson can arrange a time to get together after the ceremony.

(C) Thomas Rodman will have his Assistant Manager, Mr. Will, represent him because he cannot attend in person.

(D) Daisy & Daniel's is a company engaged in the business of fashion apparel.

（答案＆解析，詳見P198）

By Paul Chang, Staff Reporter

The Council of Labor Affairs is considering making changes to its typhoon policy guidelines. The CLA said that as of now it is inclined to require employers not to withhold wages for workers who take their mandated "typhoon leave;" and if workers are still required to be on duty during such times, they should be given extra pay. The policies have not been finalized, however.

According to current regulations, if a local government announces a day off because of typhoon, the announcement applies only to members of government agencies and schools. Whether workers working with private firms are allowed to take "typhoon leave" or not depends on their employment contracts. Even if employers give workers the day off, they are not required to pay them their regular wages.

Labor groups have been petitioning the Council of Labor Affairs since last year, demanding that when it comes to typhoon leaves laborers should be given the same treatment as civil servants. As a result, the CLA is drafting new guidelines on this matter, and said before the start of this year's typhoon season they will try to announce its new typhoon policy guidelines. The draft states that a worker can take a typhoon day off as long as the local government of his workplace, residence or the area through which he or she commutes has announced a typhoon day off, and their absence should not be regarded as absenteeism or leave of absence for personal reasons. The employer may not force the employee to make up for the absence, withhold attendance bonuses or resort to dismissal.

It is foreseeable that employers may still try to find loopholes in the new policy, and require laborers to show up for work during typhoon leaves. But since the guidelines are being made without legal basis, no fines could be given to employers that violate the guidelines. The ministry could only "encourage" employers to follow its policy guidelines.

As to how workers taking typhoon leaves will be paid is still being fiercely debated between representatives of labor and management.

---

3 July, 2009

Dear Staff Colleagues:

This e-mail serves to inform every employees of GMC that we are required to come to work on Saturday, July 18, 2009 in order to make up for the absence on Monday, 23 June, 2009 due to the typhoon leave.

Anyone who is unable to show up for work on July 18, 2009, please ask your supervisor for personal leave in advance, and please note that one day's wage will be deducted from your salary of July.

Should there be any queries, please directly contact me or any staff in Personnel Department.

Best Regards,
Cindy Brook

Manager of Personnel Department

___ 1. According to the news and the e-mail, which of the following statements is true?

(A) GMC requires laborers to show up for work during typhoon leaves.

(B) GMC tends to regard a worker's absence on a typhoon day off as absenteeism.

(C) Employers are legally forced to give workers the typhoon day off and still pay them their regular wages.

(D) GMC is a private firm rather than a government agency.

___ 2. What can we infer from the news and the e-mail?

   (A) GMC will be fined if they don't let their
       employees take typhoon leaves.
   (B) It is obvious that GMC is trying to find loopholes
       in the new typhoon policy.
   (C) Employers should give workers extra pay if
       they show up for work on typhoon leaves.
   (D) GMC forces the employees to make up for the
       absence on typhoon leaves in a disguise form.

___ 3. What have Labor groups been petitioning the
       Council of Labor Affairs for?

   (A) They require employers to hold back wages for
       workers who take typhoon leave.
   (B) They demand that the new typhoon policy
       should be made with legal basis.
   (C) They claim that when it comes to typhoon
       leaves laborers should be treated as civil
       servants.
   (D) They insist that the CLA finalize to its new
       typhoon policy before the start of this year's
       typhoon season.

____ 4. In what circumstances should GMC employees ask personal leave in advance?

(A) When they are too sick to come to work during the typhoon leave.

(B) When they are unable to show up for work to make up for the absence on typhoon leave.

(C) When the local government announces a day off because of typhoon.

(D) When they have queries about the new typhoon policy guidelines or regulations.

____ 5. What is the main purpose of the e-mail?

(A) To inform the employees of the date when they should come to work to make up for the typhoon holiday.

(B) To support the new typhoon policy guidelines announced just before the start of this year's typhoon season.

(C) To oppose the current regulations about how employees taking typhoon leaves should be paid.

(D) To encourage the employers to follow the CLA's latest typhoon policy guidelines.

（答案＆解析，詳見P202）

❸ 長文閱讀測驗

Patrick Lai,

Director of High Tech Sector, PLATINUM Ltd.

****

To: Patrick Lai, Director of High Tech Sector,
    PLATINUM Ltd.

Dear Mr. Lai,

We regret to inform you that the PLATINUM 2011 Annual Conference we scheduled on June 8-10 will be procrastinated till June 15-17 due to some internal factors. The conference, as planned, will be held in the Third Conference Hall at Agora Garden located in Xin Yi District in Taipei. You can find the attached file for the most updated conference schedule.

In addition, there will be a pre-conference workshops taking place on June 12 in the meeting room in our office building. Please set aside a little time for it out of your tight schedule.

Please accept our sincere apology for any inconvenience the procrastination may have caused you.

Thank you very much for your understanding.

Yours faithfully,
Emily

PLATINUM 2011 Annual Conference Schedule

Day 1/Wednesday 15 June 2011

14:00 – 16:30	Registration —Conference Room 201, Apollo Hall
16:30 – 17:30	Delegate Briefing (Mandatory) —Conference Room 201, Apollo Hall
17:30 – 19:00	Dinner
19:00 – 21:00	Opening Ceremony
21:00 – 21:30	Head Delegate/Faculty Advisor Reception

Day 2/Thursday 16 June 2011

09:00 – 12:00	Committee Session I
12:00 – 13:30	Lunch
13:30 – 16:30	Committee Session II
16:30 – 17:30	Head Delegate Meeting
17:30 – 19:00	Dinner
19:00 – 22:00	PLATINUM Party

Day 3/Friday 17 June 2011

09:00 – 12:00	Committee Session III
12:00 – 13:30	Lunch
13:30 – 16:30	Committee Session IV
16:30 – 17:00	Last Head Delegate Meeting
17:00 – 17:30	Closing Ceremony and Awards Presentation

(Still subject to change.)

___ 1. What is the primary purpose of the e-mail?

    (A) To announce the new employee regulations.

    (B) To cancel a scheduled annual conference.

    (C) To inform the postponement of the annual conference.

    (D) To reschedule the appointment with the director.

___ 2. What is Patrick Lai expected to do before the annual conference?

    (A) To request updated schedule for the annual conference.

    (B) To reply to the conference invitation.

    (C) To make apology for the procrastination of the conference.

    (D) To attend the pre-conference workshop.

___ 3. Which information is not included in the attached file?

(A) The time when participants are supposed to register for the conference.

(B) The rough procedures of the three-day annual conference.

(C) The list of all the participants that will show up in the conference.

(D) The exact time when the annual conference will end.

___ 4. What can we learn from the above e-mail and the schedule?

(A) The participants in the conference are probably exeoutives in the company.

(B) The conference is rescheduled probably because of the inhospitable weather.

(C) The conference serves as a celebration of the company's recent expansion.

(D) The participants are encouraged to bring their personal assistants along.

___ 5. Which of the following statements is false according to the above e-mail and schedule?

(A) The annual conference will last three days and two nights.

(B) There will be four committee sessions during the conference.

(C) The schedule attached to the e-mail is the finalized version.

(D) The location where to hold the conference remains unchanged.

（答案＆解析，詳見P206）

Dear Mr. Brown,

In response to your letter, dated March 21, querying whether it is safe to attend the 2011 International Seminar on Business and Human Rights held in Taiwan, we are confident to tell you that there is nothing you need to worry about.

We understand that you are concerned about being affected by the radiation from Japan, but according to the Atomic Energy Council, Tokyo's radiation levels are safe, let alone that of Taiwan.

There is literally no danger of radiation poisoning in Taiwan at this moment. You can relax and attend the seminar as planned. Here I attached an article to the mail, hoping to release your worry.

We'll be looking forward to welcoming you on April 15.

Best Regards,
Susan Johnson

Radioactive dust due from Japan poses no risk

According to the Atomic Energy Council (AEC), the amount of radioactive dust released from a crippled Japanese nuclear power plant that will reach Taiwan will pose no threat to human health.

Based on meteorological conditions, radioactive fallout from Japan that will reach Taiwan in the coming days will have a radiation level far below the maximum permissible level of 0.2 microsieverts per hour, and thus, will not pose a health risk.

"There is no need to panic over the radiation leak because the amount is too tiny to be harmful to human health," the director of the AEC's Department of Radiation Protection, Lee emphasized. He said the radiation level of the fallout from Japan was three-thousandths of the amount given off by a chest X-ray so that we do not have to worry about it.

Lee also said that none of the 721 food items from Japan tested since the nuclear crisis began have been found to have unsafe levels of radioactive substances.

He added that the AEC was planning to strengthen its monitoring of radiation in Taiwan by increasing the frequency of testing for radioactive substances in the air and in agricultural products and fish.

___ 1. What is the most possible purpose of Mr. Brown's visit to Taiwan?

    (A) For sightseeing.

    (B) On business.

    (C) To visit relatives.

    (D) On vacation.

___ 2. What does the article mainly discuss?

    (A) How radioactive dust released from Japan nuclear reactor is going to harm human health.

    (B) How to prevent ourselves from being affected by the radioactive dust released from Japan.

    (C) How radiation destroyed tourism industry in the neighboring countries around Japan.

    (D) How tiny the amount of radiation leak from Japan is so that it can hardly pose a health risk.

___ 3. What can we learn from the e-mail and the article?

    (A) All fish products from Japan are being banned at the moment.

    (B) The International Seminar on Business and Human Rights is being postponed.

    (C) Radioactive dust released from Japan nuclear reactor will not reach Taiwan.

    (D) AEC will strengthen its monitoring of radiation in Taiwan.

❸
長
文
閱
讀
測
驗

___ 4. Which of the following can best explain why it is safe to come to Taiwan?

(A) The radiation level of radioactive fallout from Japan is far below the maximum permissible level.

(B) All 721 food items imported from Japan will be tested after Japan's nuclear crisis.

(C) No radioactive substances have been found in the air and in agricultural products and fish.

(D) The frequency of testing for radioactive substances in the air will increase.

___ 5. What conclusion can we draw from the e-mail and the article?

(A) Taiwan cannot avoid being affected by radioactive poison.

(B) There is no need to panic over the radiation leak from Japan.

(C) Unsafe levels of radioactive substances were found in food items from Japan.

(D) The International Seminar on Business and Human Rights will be put off till the nuclear crisis is over.

（答案＆解析，詳見P210）

Hi, Linda, nice to meet you! I am Jessica, the personnel specialist from the Personnel Division. Let me introduce you the main tasks of your job. You will be playing a very important role in our office. Apart from the office chores, such as answering phones, recruiting for new hires, travel arrangements, coordinating messenger service, faxing, copying, scanning, filling, handling of sensitive HR documentation and running errands, there are quite a few things you are in charge of. To fill the position capably, you have to provide supervision to reception volunteers, take and transcribe minutes of Board and Committee meetings, type and word process documents as needed. In addition, it is also your responsibility to assume receptionist duties, greet public and refer them to appropriate staff members. You are supposed to keep lobby and front desk area clean and free from clutter. Since you have had some related working experience, you should know that you are expected to assist staff with administrative duties as requested and get through with other duties as assigned. Last but not least, you are also in charge of ordering office supplies and monitoring inventory. Well, this is probably it. You will receive your employee's card this afternoon. I hope you enjoy working with us.

___ 1. According to the speech, what job position is Linda taking on?

(A) Office assistant.

(B) Personnel specialist.

(C) Software engineer.

(D) Administration supervisor.

___ 2. Which of the following is excluded from Linda's responsibilities?

(A) To assist staff with administrative duties as requested.

(B) To maintain the cleanliness of the washrooms and the pantry.

(C) To receive guests before referring them to appropriate staff members.

(D) To recruit for new hires and running office errands.

___ 3. What can we infer from this speech?

(A) Linda had no working experience before.

(B) Linda is interviewing for a job.

(C) It is Linda's first day on the job.

(D) Linda will be working in the same division with Jessica.

___ 4. What is the purpose of the speech?

    (A) Interview a new employee.

    (B) Introduce Linda the main tasks of her job.

    (C) Introduce a new staff.

    (D) Discuss the proposal.

___ 5. According to the speech,　which statement is TRUE ?

    (A) Linda doesn't have to answer the phone.

    (B) Jessica is Linda's neighbor.

    (C) If Linda wants to fill the position capably, she has to provide supervision to reception volunteers.

    (D) Keeping lobby and front desk area clean and free from clutter is not one of Linda's responsibilities.

（答案＆解析，詳見p213）

Notice of Temporary Closure of Bon Appetit French Dining

The Royal Garden Tokyo's management confirms that the Japan Fair Trade Commission commenced an investigation at the Royal Garden Tokyo on September 10, with regard to suspected misrepresentations of the provenance of some items on the hotel's Bon Appetit restaurant menu.

The hotel management takes this matter very seriously, and has decided to suspend operations at its Bon Appetit restaurant until further notice.

The allegations refer specifically to the example of Maesawa beef fillet on the menu of Bon Appetite which was replaced with Yamagata beef fillet.

The hotel management team is currently conducting an investigation into this matter and intends to fully cooperate with the local authorities.

Royal Garden deeply regrets any inconvenience this causes its valued customers and is putting in place a series of measures to ensure there is no recurrence of these issues.

September 12, 2011
Benjamin W. Bowie
General Manager
Royal Garden Tokyo

___ 1. What information is this announcement trying to
convey to the customers?

(A) The Maesawa beef fillet on the menu of Bon
Appetite will be replaced with Yamagata beef
fillet.

(B) Japan Fair Trade Commission will hold a press
conference at Royal Garden Tokyo Hotel.

(C) Bon Appetite restaurant is going to suspend
business for rectification.

(D) Bon Appetite restaurant is accused of replacing
some items on the menu with those of different
provenances.

___ 2. According to the announcement, how does the hotel deal with the situation?

(A) They intend to make a legal claim against the false allegation.

(B) They plan to give a press conference and explain the whole story.

(C) They promise to punish those who neglected their duties severely.

(D) They suspend operations at the restaurant and conduct an investigation into this matter.

___ 3. What can we infer from this announcement?

(A) The beef fillet on Bon Appetite's menu is entirely imported from the U.S.

(B) Bon Appetite restaurant will suspend business for a period of time.

(C) Royal Garden Tokyo Hotel will surely contend with the local authorities.

(D) The Bon Appetite restaurant was ordered to suspend business with immediate effect.

___ 4. According to the announcement, the word "misrepresentation" in paragraph 1 is closest in meaning to _____.

(A) Canard.

(B) Purpose.

(C) Determination.

(D) Description.

___ 5. Which of the following is true abou this announcement?

(A) The allegations refer specifically to the example of Yamagata beef fillet on the menu of Bon Appetite which was replaced with Maesawa beef fillet.

(B) Bon Appetit French Dining will reopen on September 10th.

(C) Japan Fair Trade Commission commenced an investigation at the Royal Garden Tokyo at the end of August.

(D) Bon Appetit French Dining will be temporary close.

（答案＆解析，詳見P216）

❸
長
文
閱
讀
測
驗

Whether you call it an installment agreement, payment agreement, payment option or a payment plan, the idea is the same — you make payments on the tax you owe. That sounds like a good deal, but you can save money by paying the full amount you owe to minimize the interest and penalties you'll be charged. For those who cannot resolve their tax debt immediately, however, an installment agreement can be a reasonable payment option. Installment agreements allow for the full payment of the tax debt in smaller, more manageable amounts.

Taxpayers wishing to pay off a tax debt through an installment agreement, and owe:

- $15,000 or less in combined tax, penalties, and interest can use the Online Payment Agreement (OPA) or call the number on the bill or notice. A fill-in Request for Installment Agreement, Form A1 (PDF), is available online that can be mailed to the address on the bill.

Note: If you recently filed your income tax return and owe but have NOT yet received a bill, you can use the Online Payment Agreement to establish an installment agreement on current year returns.

- More than $15,000 in combined tax, penalties, and interest may still qualify for an installment agreement, but a Collection Information Statement, Form B3 (PDF) may need to be completed. Call the number on the bill or mail the Request for Installment Agreement, FormA1 (PDF) and Form B3 (PDF) to the address on the bill.

You will receive a written notification telling you whether your terms for an installment agreement have been accepted or if they need to be modified.

___ 1. What is this information mainly about?

    (A) How to reclaim overpaid tax.

    (B) Where to download Form A1.

    (C) How to pay tax by installments.

    (D) Where to submit Form A1 and Form B3.

___ 2. Who of the following is most likely to need this information?

(A) Someone who cannot resolve their tax debt immediately.
(B) Someone who avoids being charged for interest and penalties.
(C) Someone who wants to open a saving account in a commercial bank.
(D) Someone who tends to submit their individual tax returns by e-filing.

___ 3. In what circumstance may one receive a written notification after mailing the Request for Installment Agreement to the organization concerned?

(A) When there is no payment shows in the account for 3 months.
(B) When his/her terms for an installment agreement have been accepted.
(C) When he/she miss two payments of his/her monthly bill.
(D) If he/she signs up a 12-month payment plan but decides to pay it off in 6 months.

___ 4. According to the information, what does the word penalties refer to?

(A) Person.
(B) Salary.
(C) Principal.
(D) Punishment.

_____ 5. If you recently filed your income tax return and owe but have NOT yet received a bill, what can you do?

(A) Just ignore it.

(B) You can use the Online Payment Agreement to establish an installment agreement on current year returns.

(C) Call the bank to solve it.

(D) It doesn't mention.

（答案＆解析，詳見P219）

📝 長文閱讀 17

Dear Mrs. Kinns,

I wrote to you six weeks ago and requested that you refund me the money which I paid for a defective bread machine. I have returned the appliance and your returns department wrote me a letter acknowledging that they have received it. It is now three weeks since I received the letter. However, despite the fact that I have returned your product as specified on the purchase agreement, I have not received a replacement or a refund of my money.

I have been very patient with your company, but I cannot accept a replacement at this time because I have already purchased one as I needed a bread machine rather urgently. So could you please refund the money as soon as possible? I am sure you understand my position given the time it has taken you to respond to my request.

I am sending you a copy of the letter I received from the returns department of your company in hopes that it will help expedite refund of my money. I also trust that you will refund the NT$200 which I spent on shipping the product back to your company.

Thank you very much for your attention to this matter. I am looking forward to your prompt response.

Yours Sincerely,

Jasmine Lawrence
Jasmine Lawrence

___ 1. What is the main purpose of this letter?
   (A) To explain the reasons for the delay in an order of a bread machine.
   (B) To inform the household appliance retailer that part of the order is damaged.
   (C) To ask for a refund of money paid for a defective bread machine.
   (D) To request a replacement for the defective bread machine.

___ 2. According to the letter, what has Jasmine Lawrence received from the returns department so far?

(A) A letter which acknowledged that they had received the defective commodity.

(B) An amount of money included the refund of the bread machine plus the freight.

(C) A replacement for the commodity damaged during the transportation.

(D) The purchase agreement and an invoice.

___ 3. According to the letter, which of the following statements is not true?

(A) Jasmine Lawrence has already bought another bread machine.

(B) Jasmine Lawrence is expecting a replacement for the imperfect product.

(C) Jasmine Lawrence shipped the product back to the store as specified on the purchase agreement.

(D) Jasmine Lawrence thinks the store should pay for the transportation charges.

____ 4. According to the letter, what does the word
    "defective" in paragraph 1 mean?

    (A) Faulty.
    (B) Professional.
    (C) Perfect.
    (D) Fluent.

____ 5. Which of the following is true about about Jasmine ?

    (A) She accepts to replacement of the bread
        machine.
    (B) She wrote a letter to Mrs. Kinns last week.
    (C) She has already purchased one as she
        needed a bread machine rather urgently.
    (D) She spent $100 on shipping the product back
        to the company.

（答案＆解析，詳見P223）

📝 長文閱讀 18

Dear Ms. Sandra Wu,

We are pleased to convey that you have successfully completed three months of probation period and the Management has taken the unanimous decision to make you a permanent employee of Pioneer Book Publisher.

In view of your satisfactory performance, you have been confirmed at the position of Executive Editor at Pioneer Book Publisher and your salary has been revised to NT$33,000, with effect from 07/01/2011. You will receive your salary on or before the 5th of every month.

If you have any doubts or queries, please discuss with your supervisor.

Sincerely,

Judies Barren
Managing Director
10 June 2011.

___ 1. What is the main purpose of this letter?

    (A) To inform the recipient that she is formally employed.

    (B) To inform the recipient that she will be transferred to another division.

    (C) To inform the recipient that her performance at work is barely satisfactory.

    (D) To explain to the recipient the reason why she got laid off.

___ 2. When will Ms. Sandra Wu officially become a regular worker at Pioneer Book Publisher?

    (A) From the 10th day of June in 2011.

    (B) From the first day of July in 2011.

    (C) From the date of this letter.

    (D) After she discusses with her supervisor.

___ 3. Which is NOT mentioned in this letter?

    (A) Where Sandra Wu is employed.

    (B) How long has Sandra been working at this company.

    (C) How much Sandra is paid per month.

    (D) The name of Sandra's supervisor.

_____ 4. What is the best title for the letter?

(A) A temporary Employment Notice

(B) A Welcome Party Announcement

(C) A Permanent Employment Letter

(D) A New Company Ad

_____ 5. According to the letter, which statement is TRUE?

(A) The HR Manager wrote this letter.

(B) Judy is the executive editor at Pioneer Book Publisher .

(C) Sandra's salary has been revised over NT$35000.

(D) Judy is satisfied with Sandra's performance.

（答案＆解析，詳見P225）

Dear Customers,

Unfortunately, effective from August 1st we must raise the price on toilet/facial tissues. The new prices will be:

- toilet tissues 　 12 packs 　 NT$150
　Facial tissues 　50 packs 　 NT$99

We regret that we have to pass on this increase, but it will allow us to continue to provide high value toilet/facial tissues to our customers. This means that we will continue to offer high quality products with competitive prices.

We appreciate your business and look forward to serving you in the future.

Regards,
Lynn Farmer
Manager of Star Mart Supermarket

___ 1. What can we learn from the announcement?

(A) There will be a clearance sale.

(B) There are no tissues in stock.

(C) The store doesn't accept on-line orders.

(D) The store will raise the price on tissues.

___ 2. What information is this announcement trying to convey to the customers?

(A) The anniversary sale will start from August 1st.

(B) The price in certain commodities will increase from August 1st .

(C) The store will close from August 1st for a month.

(D) The store will stop offering toilet/facial tissues from August 1st .

___ 3. Which of the following is not mentioned in the announcement?

(A) The reason for the price increase.

(B) Items that will have a rise in price.

(C) The effective date of the price increase.

(D) The name of the store manager.

___ 4. According to the announcement, what is the word
"competitive" closest in meaning to?

(A) Lower prices.
(B) Expensive.
(C) Passive.
(D) Luxurious.

___ 5. What would be a good title for this announcement?

(A) New Supermarket Promotion
(B) Raising the Price Announcement
(C) Sale and Clearance Ad
(D) New Products to Sell Online

（答案＆解析，詳見P228）

Hello Sunday's ®　Treat Yourself Well

Buy One Entrée,
Get One Free.

Not for resale. Valid at participating Hello Sunday's ® Restaurant for dine-in-only. Not replaceable if lost or stolen. One coupon, per table, per visit. Not valid in conjunction with any other offer. Tax and gratuity not included. Unless required by law, certificate cannot be redeemed for cash or used to pay gratuities. Offer expires December 31, 2011. Offer valid in Taiwan. Discount applies to item of equal or lesser value. ©2011 Hello Sunday's Inc.

Coupon Code: HSENTREE30669　VALID: 01/12/11-31/12/11

___ 1. When does this coupon effective come into effect?

(A) From December in 2011.
(B) Until December 1st in 2011.
(C) From December 31 in 2011.
(D) Not mentioned.

___ 2. Which of the following statements is NOT TRUE?

(A) This coupon is only accepted in Hello Sunday's Restaurants located in Taiwan.

(B) The customers can have a takeout entrée for free by showing this coupon.

(C) This coupon cannot be used in combination with any other preferential activities.

(D) The coupon holder cannot sell the coupon even he/she doesn't plan to dine in Hello Sunday's.

___ 3. What can a customer do if his/her coupon is lost or stolen?

(A) Ask for a replacement by showing his/her ID card.

(B) Demand for a compensation from the restaurant.

(C) He/She can do nothing but accept the truth.

(D) Buy another coupon from an internet auction site.

___ 4. What type of store is Hello Sunday's?

(A) A drugstore.

(B) A grocery.

(C) A supermarket.

(D) A restaurant.

___ 5. Neil books a table for four. How many coupon can he use?

(A) Four coupons.
(B) Three coupons.
(C) Two coupons.
(D) One coupon.

（答案＆解析，詳見P230）

📝 長文閱讀 21

Dear Mr. Tom Chang,

We had been hoping that during this difficult period of reorganization we could keep all of our employees with the company. Unfortunately, things don't turn out the way we want.

It is with regret, consequently, that we must inform you that we will be unable to utilize your services after June 30, 2011. We have been pleased with the qualities you have exhibited during your tenure of employment with us, and will be sorry to lose you as an employee of the company.

Please accept our best wishes for your future.

Department of Personnel Management

_____ 1. What is the main purpose of the letter?

    (A) To apologize for inconvenience caused by their mistakes.

    (B) To congratulate Tom Chang on his promotion.

    (C) To offer Tom Chang an opportunity to job-hop to their company.

    (D) To inform Tom Chang that he has been dismissed from his job.

_____ 2. According to the letter, when will the company terminate the employment of Tom?

    (A) From July 1st , 2011.

    (B) From June 30, 2011.

    (C) A month later.

    (D) Not mentioned.

_____ 3. In the second paragraph of the letter, the word "utilize" is closest in meaning to

    (A) apply.

    (B) supply.

    (C) refuse.

    (D) return.

___ 4. Why did the department of personnel management manager fire Tom Chang?

(A) He wasn't satisfied with Tom's performance.

(B) The company faced a difficult period.

(C) Tom went to work late recently.

(D) He's argued with Tom for times.

___ 5. According to the letter, which of the following sentences is true?

(A) All of the employees with the company lost their job.

(B) Tom would be unable to utilize his services after receiving this letter.

(C) The supervisor has been pleased with the qualities Tom has exhibited during his tenure of employment.

(D) Tom decided to quit the job.

（答案＆解析，詳見p232）

Type of Supply	Duration of Suspension	Affected Area / Buildings	Reasons of Suspension
Fresh Water	22:00 hr. on 25 March 2011 (Friday) to 06:00 hr. on 26 March 2011 (Saturday)	Taipei City- The suspension will affect some premises at Da An District and Xin Yi District	Alteration work on water mains to be carried out

Please be informed that water supply to the areas as shown in the above list has been temporarily suspended. We apologize for any inconvenience caused.

Please note that the supply may be restored earlier than estimated or the suspension of supply may have to be extended in case of unforeseen circumstances or emergencies. Please call 0800-345-678, our 24-hour Customer Service Hotline, for further information.

___ 1. What is the main purpose of this notice?

   (A) To announce a water suspension.

   (B) To apply for unemployment benefit.

   (C) To refuse to attend a conference.

   (D) To notify a power restriction.

___ 2. How long will the suspension last?

   (A) For twenty-four hours.

   (B) For eighteen hours.

   (C) For eight hours.

   (D) For thirty-six hours.

___ 3. According to the notice, what is the reason for suspending the water supply?

   (A) To perform water quality testing.

   (B) To carry out alteration work on water mains.

   (C) To put water-saving policy into effect.

   (D) To punish users for not paying the water bills.

____ 4. Which of the following situations is not mentioned in the notice?

(A) The water supply may be restored earlier than estimated.

(B) The suspension may be extended due to unpredictable conditions.

(C) Areas aside from that are mentioned in the list may be affected without warning.

(D) Customer Service Hotline is provided for people who enquire further information.

____ 5. If you need any further information, what can you do?

(A) Fax the Customer Service.

(B) Call the Customer Service Hotline.

(C) Search and browse the Internet to find the answer.

(D) Call the cell phone.

（答案＆解析，詳見P235）

📝 **長文閱讀 23**

Dear Sir,

My name is Brian Lin and I would like to book a room, full board, in your hotel for three nights.

My wife and I will be arriving on January 15, 2011, Saturday at approximately four p.m. Departure will be on January 18, 2011, Tuesday at ten a.m.

We prefer a double room with a lake view. If there are no double rooms available, a twin room will be fine.

Please arrange our room far away from any entertainment facilities and we need an internet connection in our room.

The following are my contact information.
Cell phone number: 0912-345-678
Fax number: 076663888

Brian Lin

Dear Mr. Lin,

This letter is the confirmation of your reservation at the Holiday Inn Resort. Your confirmation number is 6088. You are confirmed for a stay of three nights, from January 15 through January 18, 2011, in a room with a double bed. The rate is NT$5600 per night. Regrettably, there are no rooms available with a lake view.

Since this is a guaranteed reservation, you must cancel at least 24 hours before your planned arrival to receive a refund. Thanks for choosing to stay with us. We look forward to your arrival.

Best Regards,
Holiday Inn Resort

____ 1. What is the main purpose of Brian Lin's letter?

    (A) To cancel a room reservation.

    (B) To make a room reservation.

    (C) To put off an appointment.

    (D) To respond to an invitation.

___ 2. Which of the following is not the special need that Brian specifies in his letter?

(A) To stay in a room far away from any entertainment facilities.

(B) To stay in a room with an internet connection.

(C) To stay in a double room where he can enjoy the city view.

(D) To stay in the hotel with all meals provided.

___ 3. When are Brian and his wife planning to leave the hotel?

(A) Around four p.m. on January 15.

(B) Before noon on January 18.

(C) In the afternoon of January 18.

(D) After eleven in the morning of January 15.

___ 4. What can we infer from the confirmation letter?

(A) The hotel doesn't provide internet connection service.

(B) The hotel doesn't provide breakfast.

(C) All the rooms with a lake view are booked.

(D) The hotel doesn't accept cancellation.

_____ 5. If Brian wants to cancel his reservation and receive a refund, when does he need to contact the hotel at the latest?

(A) Two days before his planned arrival.

(B) One day before his planned arrival.

(C) Half day before his planned arrival.

(D) Two hours before his planned arrival.

（答案＆解析，詳見P237）

📝 長文閱讀 24

Dear Mr. Chuang,

B&R is pleased to offer you a job as a Technology Coordinator. We trust that your knowledge, skills and experience will be among our most valuable assets.

Should you accept this job offer, per company policy you'll be eligible to receive the following beginning on your hire date.

- **Salary:** Annual gross starting salary paid in monthly installments by direct deposit.
- **Performance Bonuses:** Up to three percent of your annual gross salary, paid quarterly by direct deposit
- **Benefits:** Standard, B&R-provided benefits for salaried-exempt employees, including the following

- Three Chinese festival bonus
- Labor and health insurance
- Sick leave, marital leave, maternal leave, etc.
- Vacation and personal days

You will find the employment agreement attached to this mail. Please peruse it before you sign it on your start date.

Best Regards,
B&R Human Resource Management

EMPLOYMENT AGREEMENT

By and between <u>B&R Co. Ltd.</u> referred to as "Company", and <u>Max Chuang</u> referred to as "the Employee".

The Company employs Employee and Employee hereby agrees to be employed on the following terms and conditions:

1. DUTIES: Employee agrees to perform the duties set out herein:

- research information regarding computer operating systems

- review current operating systems, make changes to systems and even may develop operating systems • maintaining contact with customers, project managers and other company employees
- administrative duties
- prepare reports, graphs, charts and evaluations throughout the daily job routines
- employee shall perform such further duties as are customarily performed by one holding such position in other businesses of the same or similar nature as that engaged in by Company.

2. COMPENSATION: In consideration of the foregoing, Company shall pay Employee a salary of NT$910,000 per year, for Employee's services.

3. DURATION OF EMPLOYMENT: Employee's agreement shall remain in effect until it is terminated by either party, commencing on July 1, 2011.

4. TERMINATION: This agreement may be terminated earlier upon (1) death of Employee or illness or incapacity that prevents Employee from performing his/her duties for a period of more than three weeks in any calendar year and (2) breach of the agreement by Employee. Such

option shall be exercised by Employer giving a notice to Employee by certified mail, addressed to him in care of employer. With such notice, this agreement shall cease and come to an end seven days after in which the notice is mailed.

5. MISCELLANEOUS: (1) Employee agrees not to disclose any of Company's trade marks during or after the employment. (2) In the event of any dispute over this agreement, it shall be resolved through binding arbitration under the rules of the Arbitration Association of the ROC.

In witness whereof, both parties have executed this agreement at B&R Co. Ltd., on July 1, 2011.

Company

_____

Employee

_____

___ 1. What can we learn from the above letter and document?

(A) B&R is offering Max Chuang a job opportunity.

(B) B&R is recruiting Max Chuang from his current company.

(C) B&R is congratulating Max Chuang on getting a promotion.

(D) B&R is inviting Max Chuang to remain in office.

___ 2. According to the agreement, which of the following is excluded from a technology coordinator's duties at B&R?

(A) To research information regarding computer operating systems.

(B) To implement the district technology plan.

(C) To maintaining contact with customers.

(D) To prepare reports throughout the daily job routines.

___ 3. According to the agreement, in what circumstance shall B&R terminate the employment with Max Chuang?

(A) Max Chuang isn't able to work for over three weeks because of sickness.

(B) Max Chuang asks for sick leave for a week.

(C) Max Chuang asks for marital leave on his start date.

(D) Max Chuang doesn't get his salary on schedule.

___ 4. What benefit is not mentioned in the letter from the Human Resource Management?

(A) Year-end bonus.

(B) Wedding vacation.

(C) Funeral leave.

(D) Health insurance.

___ 5. How often will the company pay for Max Chuang's services at work?

(A) Once every three months.

(B) Once every other weeks.

(C) Once a week.

(D) Once a month.

（答案＆解析，詳見P240）

Joan's Apparel Shop Order Form
Fax order Line: 993-660-2211

Quantity	Item name	Model No.	Size	Color	Item Price
2	tops	TP3066557	6	beige	190
1	skirt	SK2255369	6.5	brown	390
1	shorts	SO1002538	6.5	black	290
1	swimwear	SW0033501	S	pink	480
				Sub-Total:	1540
☐ ordinary parcel – add $80 NTD				Shipping:	120
☑ express delivery – add 120 NTD					
Total:					1660

Contact name	Amanda Hsiao
Phone number	978-363-5400
Contact address	17 Prospect St. W. Newbury, Mass 01985
Shipping address	the same as above
Email address	Amanda1013_hsiao@gmail.com
Method of Payment	☐ Master charge or Visa 　Your credit card no. 　☐☐☐☐☐☐☐☐☐☐☐☐☐☐☐☐ 　Valid Date 　☐☐☐☐☐☐ 　<u>d</u> <u>d</u> <u>m</u> <u>m</u> <u>y</u> <u>y</u> ☐ Bank Transfer ☑ Cash On Delivery
Order date	2011/4/21

To: Ms. Amanda Hsiao
From: Joan's Apparel Shop
Subject: Order #10667

Dear Ms. Hsiao,

Thank you very much for ordering our commodities. With regret, we have to inform you that some of the items you requested in your order on April 21 (order #10667) are currently out of stock. Our supplier told us that those items will not be available until the end of next month, May 31, at the earliest. Those items are listed below:

1 skirt size   6.5   brown
1 swimwear size   S   pink

Please let us know if you wish to cancel any of the above items due to the delay in availability as soon as possible, otherwise, we will have your order delivered by overnight express when they arrive. You should be able to receive them by June 1st at the latest. As for the remaining items you ordered, we will have them sent by five p.m. today, and they should arrive at your shipping address by noon tomorrow.

Please accept our sincere apology for all the inconvenience this may have caused you.

Best Regards,
Joan's Apparel Shop

_____ 1. What is the main purpose of this e-mail?

    (A) To inform the customer that her credit card is invalid.

    (B) To inform the customer that her order has been cancelled.

    (C) To inform the customer that part of her order is out of stock.

    (D) To inform the customer that the shop will be closed for a while.

_____ 2. How is the customer going to pay for her order?

    (A) By cash.

    (B) By credit card.

    (C) By installment.

    (D) By mortgage.

_____ 3. In what circumstance should Ms. Hsiao contact Joan's Apparel Shop as soon as possible?

    (A) In the event that she wish to cancel the entire order.

    (B) In the event that she wish to cancel the items currently unavailable.

    (C) In the event that she is unable to pay by credit card.

    (D) In the event that her commodities are damaged during the transportation.

___ 4. How much will the customer have to pay when she receive her first shipment?

    (A) $790 NTD.

    (B) $1,540 NTD.

    (C) $1,660 NTD.

    (D) $870 NTD.

___ 5. Which of the following information is not mentioned in the above form and e-mail?

    (A) The location of the apparel shop.

    (B) The contact number of the customer.

    (C) The fax order number of the shop.

    (D) The date the customer placed the order.

（答案＆解析，詳見244）

Dear Employees,

We are pleased to announce that we will be having our company outing on March 31, 2011 to celebrate the pleasant performance that everyone did for the past year. The company outing not only serves as the company's celebration of its recent expansion, but also to reward all employees for your hard work that made the company a top service provider in the industry.

We are encouraging you to bring your family members as the company outing also serves the company's family event. Games, raffles, and other activities will fill the day. For the confirmation of your attendance, please approach Anna or any staff in Event Planning Division or directly reply to this letter.

Regards,

Anna Clarkson
Event Planning Division

Dear Anna,

Thank you for your notification letter about the company outing. I am glad to have such a good opportunity to meet people of other sections and departments as well as develop a wider circle of friends. It's also good news that I can take my family to join the company outing with me. I'm just wondering whether there is limit for the number of participants. If there isn't, I would like to take all members of my family, namely my parents, my wife, my two children, my brother and my sister-in-law and their three kids with me. If I can't bring all of them, please let me know as early as possible.

I appreciate your prompt response.

Jack Harrlson

Staff Editor of
Research & Development Department

_____ 1. What is the main purpose of Jack Harrison's letter?

(A) To inform the Event Planning Division that he is unable to participate in the company outing.

(B) To ask for the participants limitation for each employee to the company outing.

(C) To request for detailed activity arrangement for the company outing.

(D) To suggest a good place for company outing to the Event Planning Division.

_____ 2. Which of the following information is not given in the notification letter?

(A) The purpose of the company outing.

(B) The date on which the company outing is held.

(C) The place where they are going for the company outing.

(D) The sponsoring department of the company outing.

_____ 3. What does Jack Harrison expect Anna Clarkson to tell him in her response?

(A) If there is limit for the number of participants.

(B) Whether he has to hand in any payment for the event.

(C) How long the company outing is going to last.

(D) Whether he has to ask for personal leave if he is unable to show up for the company outing.

___ 4. How many people is Jack Harrison thinking to bring with him to the company outing?

(A) Ten.

(B) Nine.

(C) Eleven.

(D) Not mentioned.

___ 5. What can we infer from the above e-mails?

(A) The company outing is held once a year.

(B) The company's business achievement for the past year was barely satisfactory.

(C) The company might have just opened branches recently.

(D) The company is thinking to reduce half of their staff.

（答案＆解析，詳見P248）

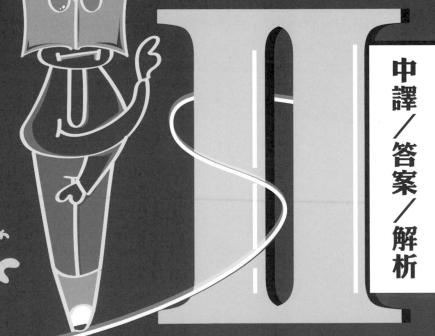

Part II

中譯／答案／解析

Chapter 1 單句填空題

中譯 & 解析

答案	題目中譯	解題攻略
1. **(C)**	如果會議有延後或任何變動，請盡快與我聯繫。 (A) 將有 (B) 應該有 **(C) 有** (D)（曾經）有	假設語氣中，if 引導的條件子句時態為現在簡單式，故選C。
2. **(A)**	隨函附上本公司最新的護膚產品型錄。若您需要更多資訊或是試用品，請不吝告知。 **(A) 隨函附上** (B) 提供 (C) 插入 (D) 供應	enclose 為「隨信附上」的意思。這裡完整的句子應該是 The document which is enclosed with the letter …，此處的先行詞及關係代名詞＋be 動詞通常予以省略，而 with the letter 也因顯而易見而省略不贅述。
3. **(C)**	感謝您給予任何意見，好讓我們研發出更能符合顧客需求的產品。 (A) 忽略 (B) 吻合 **(C) 符合** (D) 相符合	meet 有「滿足、符合」之意，依前文文意可知此處應在表達「符合顧客之需求」。conform 通常與介系詞 to 或with 合用；tally 後面亦需有介系詞 with 。故以 C 為正解。

答案	題目中譯	解題攻略
4. **(A)**	我們非常重視過去幾年與您的合作，並希望能繼續提供您最好的服務。 **(A) 提供** (B) 援助 (C) 感謝 (D) 使免受	企業的合作乃一種供需行為，因此可知 B、C 與 D 皆非適合的選項。provide someone with something 則表示「提供某物給某人」，因此選 A。
5. **(C)**	得知布魯克先生和其他幾百名員工在公司縮編時被裁員的消息讓人很難過。 (A) 晉升 (B) 加薪 **(C) 裁員** (D) 放逐	由 sad 這個字可知 that 後面引導的子句應有負面含意，故可不考慮選項 A 與 B。exile 表示「放逐、流亡」，不適合用於公司裁員，故以 C 為正解。

答案	題目中譯	解題攻略
6. (C)	恕我直言，若是一間公司員工流動率很高的話，公司本身一定有什麼問題。 (A) 向心力 (B) 福利 **(C) 流動率** (D) 諮詢	with all due respect 為禮貌地表示不同意見時所用的片語，表示「恕我直言」之意。由句中的 problem 可知此為一有負面意含的句子，故可先刪除選項 A 與 B；一般不會以 high 來形容 employee counseling「員工諮詢」，故亦非正解。employee turnover 為「員工流動率」之意，一般會以企業的員工流動率高低來判定一家企業的經營績效，故選 C。
7. (A)	在幫你加薪之前，我們必須先評估你的工作表現。 **(A) 評估** (B) 計算 (C) 捨棄 (D) 仔細考慮	abandon 為「放棄」之意，不符合文意，故不考慮 C。calculate 必須用在與數字的計算上；deliberate 則表示「深思熟慮」，後面會接介系詞 on 或 about。evaluate 則有「評估、評價」之意，故選 A。

答案	題目中譯	解題攻略
8. **(B)**	羅倫斯先生，我必須提醒您如果您要修改訂單內容，會產生一筆手續費。 (A) 取消 **(B) 手續** (C) 入場 (D) 註冊	此乃與訂單有關之費用，可先將選項 C 與 D 刪除。由文意可知，對方是要修改訂單內容而非取消訂單，故選項 A 亦不適用，應以選項 B 為正解。
9. **(B)**	既然這個團隊成員都是從本公司各部門精心挑選出來的精英，我相信他們一定能不負眾望，達成任務。 (A) 打敗 **(B) 達到** (C) 違背 (D) 紮根	「不負眾望」可用片語 live up to one's expectations 來表示；根據文意應選 B。 get the better of…意為「打敗」；go against … 則為「反對、違背」之意；take root in… 表示「紮根於……」。
10. **(B)**	有關本公司財務經理挪用公款的傳聞早已經傳遍整個辦公室。 (A) 宣傳 **(B) 流傳** (C) 傳染 (D) 入侵	由主詞為 rumor（謠言、傳聞）可判斷選項 C 與 D 的動詞不適用而不予考慮。一般對於謠言不使用 advertise（宣傳、廣告）這個動詞，而是會使用 circulate（傳播、散佈）這個動詞，故選 B。

❶ 單句填空題—中譯 & 解析

答案	題目中譯	解題攻略
11. (A)	本公司與歐美許多公司都有業務往來，因此所有員工都必須能説流利的英語及法語。 **(A) 必須的** (B) 檢查 (C) 有偏見的 (D) 自願的	前文説明了公司的業務對象，可知後文在表達員工所需具備的必要條件，be required to do 意為「必須做某事」，其他選項均不符合題意，因此選 A。
12. (D)	所有職員請於十點在會議室集合。我們將舉行緊急會議。 (A) 集中 (B) 專注 (C) 積聚 **(D) 集合**	centralize 表示「使中心化」；concentrate 表示「專注」，後面多接介系詞 on；accumulate 則表示「積累」之意。「使人集合於某處」多用 assemble 這個字。可知應選 D。
133 (C)	據説勞工們正聯合起來要爭取他們的權益。 (A) 對抗 (B) 到達 **(C) 爭取** (D) 競爭	stand against 有「反對」之意，與常理不符；set foot on 表到達，後面經常接「地點」；compete against 表示「與某人對抗」，亦與文意不符。fight for 表示「爭取、為某事奮鬥」，是為正解。

答案	題目中譯	解題攻略
14. **(A)**	主管與部屬之間良好的溝通是愉快的工作環境所不可或缺的。 **(A) 溝通** (B) 對質 (C) 同意 (D) 干擾	依文意可不考慮選項 B 及D 等帶有負面意義的字彙，agreement 表示「協議；同意」，與文意不符，以選項(A) communication 為最適當的解釋。
15. **(C)**	較低的勞工成本讓中國在生產製造產品上有相對優勢。 (A) 購買 (B) 進口 **(C) 生產** (D) 聯絡	題目中提到 lower labor cost（較低的勞工成本），可知與產品生產有關，故依文意選C。
16. **(D)**	為了能與他們的產品競爭，我們必須降低我們商品的市價。 (A) 刪除 (B) 拒絕 (C) 取消 **(D) 競爭**	依句中 lower the market price （降低市價）可判斷目的乃提高競爭力。選項的四個動詞片語中只有選項 D 符合邏輯。
17. **(B)**	這兩家公司在記者會上宣佈了他們的合作計畫。 (A) 約會 **(B) 會議** (C) 訪談 (D) 集會	press conference 為一常用片語，乃「記者會」之意，故以B 為正解。

❶ 單句填空題 — 中譯 & 解析

答案	題目中譯	解題攻略
18. **(D)**	看過約翰的說明之後，我們必須承認他非常勝任這份工作。 (A) 決定 (B) 申請 (C) 戰勝 **(D) 承認**	選項 A、B 與 C 皆與文意不符，可直接刪除不予考慮。acknowledge 意思同 admit，表示「承認……」，故選 D。
19. **(C)**	湯尼因為洩漏公司機密文件而被開除了。 (A) 自信的 (B) 讚賞的 **(C) 機密的** (D) 經典的	句中的片語 leak out 乃「洩漏出去」之意。confidential document 表示「機密文件」其他形容詞皆不適用，故選 C。
20. **(D)**	為了將會議控制在三十分鐘內，我們必須將討論重點集中在主要議題上。 (A) 預防 (B) 關閉 (C) 控制 **(D) 限制**	confine ... to... 表示「將……限制在某個時間或程度內」之意；依文意應以 D 為正解。prevent「預防」通常與 from 合用，表示「阻止某事」。
21. **(A)**	如果你不遵守休假規定，可能會被革職。 **(A) 規定** (B) 條件 (C) 情況 (D) 法規	leave provisions 表示「休假法規」。legislation 通常指「立法、法律」，並不適用於此。

答案	題目中譯	解題攻略
22. **(A)**	這項企劃的失敗是他犯下的那個無法挽救的錯誤所造成的。 **(A) 因……的結果而起的** (B) 結果 (C) 結果 (D) 結果、影響	表示「因……的結果而起」可用 be consequent on …、be the result of…、be the outcome of…，而 effect 多用於 have an effect on …，表示「對……起影響」，因此可知此處應選 A。
23. **(C)**	恭喜！你的產品宣傳提案已經被採用了。 (A) 適應 (B) 排除 **(C) 採用** (D) 取消	由 congratulations 可知後文應為正面的內容，故選項 B 與 D 可不予考慮。主詞為 proposal（提案），選項 C 會比 A 來得適當，故選 C。
24. **(A)**	據謠傳，這兩間公司將會合併成一間大企業。 **(A) 合併** (B) 分開 (C) 連結 (D) 解散	由句中的 two（二）及 single（單一的）可判斷這句在表示「二合為一」，因此只需考慮選項 A 與 C。connect 可表示兩者連結，但沒有合而為一的意思，merge 則有「使（公司）合併」之意，故以 A 為最適當的解釋。

答案	題目中譯	解題攻略
25. **(B)**	要達成我們期望的目標，還有很多問題需要全力對付。 (A) 滿足的 **(B) 應付** (C) 爭辯 (D) 來龍去脈	由 to 可知此處應為動詞，故可先刪去選項 A（content 為形容詞）與 D（context 為名詞）。片語 contend with …意為「應付、處理（問題）」，而 contest 則有「爭奪、競爭」之意。由 to 之前的受詞 problem 可知選項 B 應為正解。
26. **(C)**	根據這篇報導，連續的旱災使得農產品的價格不斷上漲。 (A) 可能的 (B) 固定的 **(C) 連續的** (D) 歷史的	由 have been increasing 可知農產品價格上漲乃一持續發生的既定事實，故選項 A 與 D 可先刪去不考慮；drought（乾旱）為一氣候現象，不會以 regular 來形容，應以選項 C：continual（持續的）為正解。
27. **(B)**	我們已經收到向貴公司訂購的麵包機了，但很遺憾地要告訴您這台機器的品質讓人相當不滿意。 (A) 喜愛 **(B) 遺憾** (C) 推斷、應該 (D) 很少	由第二句 that 子句中的 unsatisfactory（令人不滿的）可知這並非一個好消息，因此選項 A 無須考慮；I suppose … 為表示「我想……」的用法，並不適用於此；頻率副詞 seldom 亦與此句的文意無關。regret 乃委婉表示「遺憾、可惜」之意，故為正解。

答案	題目中譯	解題攻略
28. **(A)**	懷特先生已經和麥可在會議室裡談了好幾個小時了。 **(A) 談話** (B) 保存 (C) 集會 (D) 說服	convene 與 convince 均為及物動詞，不需介系詞 with，故可刪除不考慮；conserve 不符句意，亦非正解；converse with somebody 表示「與某人交談」，故選 A。
29. **(C)**	員工們很合作，加班把那個案子及時完成了。 (A) 同意的 (B) 相互的 **(C) 合作的** (D) 自私的	由句意可知選項中唯有 cooperative（合作的）這個形容詞適用於句子中，故選C。 agreeable 表示同意，後面需以介系詞 to 接名詞或做不定詞。mutual 表「互相的、彼此的」，後面需接一般名詞。
30. **(B)**	聽說公司將為更新辦公室的電腦設備編列五十萬元的預算。 (A) 聯合抵制 **(B) 編列預算** (C) 平衡 (D) 提議	依文意可刪除不符的選項 A 及C；propose 這個動詞的主詞應為人；budget … for... 乃表示「為某事編列預算」之用法，故選 B。

答案	題目中譯	解題攻略
31. **(C)**	身為主管，你應該對你的部下一視同仁。 (A) 限制 (B) 異議 **(C) 歧視** (D) 情緒	「對……一視同仁」可用片語 treat … without discrimination 來表示。discrimination 意為「歧視、不公平待遇」，故以 C 為正解。
32. **(D)**	我們將為下個月即將退休的一位資深同事舉辦歡送會。 (A) 喬遷慶宴 (B) 歡迎的 (C) 團聚 **(D) 送別的**	由句中 retire（退休）一字可知派對的性質應為送別派對，故選 D。
33. **(C)**	口譯者錯誤的翻譯為兩方帶來極大的誤解。 (A) 解決 (B) 減少 **(C) 引起** (D) 甦醒	由 faulty（錯誤的）一字可判斷此為負面句子，因此選項 A 與 B 可不考慮；選項 D：come around 意為「甦醒或改變立場」，與文意不符，亦可刪除。bring about 有「引起、帶來」之意，符合文意，故為正解。

答案	題目中譯	解題攻略
34. **(A)**	要為國際性的公司工作，你得克服語言的障礙。 **(A) 為了** (B) 只要 (C) 完成 (D) 甚至於	觀前後文可判斷 work for an international company（為國際性公司工作）乃 overcome language barrier（克服語言障礙）之目的；in order to 有「為了……」之意，因此選 A。
35. **(B)**	公司裡很少人知道布魯斯先生要去馬爾地夫度年假。 (A) 母親的 **(B) 一年一次的** (C) 每天的 (D) 社會的	maternal leave 為「產假」，不適用於主詞 Mr. Bruce，故不考慮。annual leave 為「年度休假」，亦可用 annual vacation 表示。選項 C 與 D 均不適用，故以 B 為正解。
36. **(A)**	我們公司的休假政策相當有彈性。這表示你能更靈活地安排你的休假。 **(A) 靈活地** (B) 謹慎地 (C) 聚精會神地 (D) 無理地	由前文的 elastic（有彈性的）一字，可知後文的副詞以 flexibly 最能與其相對應，故選 A。

答案	題目中譯	解題攻略
37. **(B)**	根據本公司人事規章，在你成為正式員工之前會有三個月的試用期。 (A) 正常的 **(B) 固定的** (C) 平常的 (D) 平凡的	表示「正式員工」，有permanent staff、full-time employees、regular workers、regular employees等幾種方式。regular 有「穩定的、固定的；常規的」之意，其他選項均不適用在此，故選 B。
38. **(A)**	總經理出差時，柏頓先生將會代理他的職務。 **(A) 堡壘** (B) 領域 (C) 立場 (D) 呼吸	hold the fort 為表示「代為負責、暫時代理以應付緊急情況」之片語，故選 A。
39. **(C)**	別擔心。您所訂購的肉品在運送過程中將會被保存在我們貨車上的冷藏裝置中。 (A) 翻譯 (B) 傳送 **(C) 運送** (D) 委託	選項 A 與 D 均與題意無關，可不予考慮。transmission 通常用來指「訊息、節目等」的傳播；transportation 則指「物件」的運送或搬運等。由 order（訂購）及 in our truck（在貨車內）可判定此處應選 C。

答案	題目中譯	解題攻略
40. **(A)**	所有的面試官都同意克里夫小姐完全符合做一名空服員所具備的所有條件。 **(A) 滿足** (B) 伴隨 (C) 有能力的 (D) 命令、要求	這裡需要一個動詞，因此選項C 可先刪除。accompany 則是用來表示「陪同；與……同時發生」之意，不符句意，故不選。qualification 指「限定條件」，表達「符合條件」，選項中以 A 最適當。
41. **(C)**	莎莉自從升任總經理之後就極少休假，希望她不要過度工作而累垮了自己。 (A) 興奮 (B) 混淆 **(C) 精疲力盡** (D) 厭煩	由 rarely has a day off（難有一天休假）可知工作時間很長，故可推知此處適合的動詞為 exhaust，故選 C。exhaust oneself from overwork 意為「過度工作而疲勞」。
42. **(D)**	據調查，有九成的顧客願意繼續與我們往來，這都是拜我們銷售團隊出色的顧客服務所賜。 (A) 關於 (B) 使 (C) 由於 **(D) 根據**	由文意可知這句是在敘述調查顯示的結果，故選 D。

答案	題目中譯	解題攻略
43. **(B)**	恕我直言，我真的認為你應該訂定較實際並且可預期達成的目標。 (A) 踢 **(B) 達成** (C) 完成 (D) 來	這裡所需的動詞，其受詞為先行詞之前的 goal（目標）；表示「達成目標」動詞用achieve，故選 B。
44. **(A)**	要不是老闆跟我介紹，我都不知道史密斯先生曾是我們的股東之一。 **(A) 不 (過去式)** (B) 不該 (C) 不必 (D) 還沒（過去完成式）	連接詞 until 前後的時態必須一致，故選過去簡單式 didn't。
45. **(B)**	可否請你的助理將所有的宣傳資料準備好，明天前寄給我一份當參考？ (A) 研討會 **(B) 參考** (C) 差異 (D) 偏愛	for reference 為表示「作為參考」之意，其他選項為拼字相似的單字，需小心混淆。

答案	題目中譯	解題攻略
46. (A)	員工們如預期地反對週末上班。 **(A) 反對** (B) 拒絕 (C) 不情願 (D) 抱怨	由空格後所接為動名詞 having，而選項 B 與 C 的不定詞均需接原形動詞，可刪除不考慮；選項 D：complained 後面須有介系詞 about，亦不適用。rebell at 後面可接名詞或動名詞，表示「反對……」之意，故以 A 為正解。
47. (B)	工廠必須在一週內回收所有含非法成分的產品。 (A) 取消 **(B) 召回** (C) 再教育 (D) 拘留	依文意可知此句在表示「召回產品」，故選 B。
48. (A)	不好意思。可否給我支付款項的發票，讓我可以向公司請款。 **(A) 發票** (B) 批准 (C) 契約 (D) 申請	由 apply for the company expense「報公帳」，可知這裡需要的單字應為 invoice（發票），故選 A。

答案	題目中譯	解題攻略
49. **(C)**	為了歡迎新總經理上任，企劃部上周末辦了盛大的歡迎會。 (A) 展示會 (B) 報告 **(C) 歡迎會** (D) 研討會	由 welcome（歡迎某人）可知企劃部所安排的應是一場歡迎會，故選 C。
50. **(A)**	現在真的不是辭掉工作的好時機，因為景氣不好要找工作是很困難的。 **(A) 經濟萎縮** (B) 壓力 (C) 試用期 (D) 消遣	此題是考字彙，由文意可知對「找工作不利」的情況應為經濟不景氣時期，故以選項 A 最適當。
51. **(B)**	身為一個稱職的接線生，必須記住辦公室裡每一個人的分機號碼。 (A) 登記 **(B) 分機** (C) 庫存 (D) 序號	此題是考字彙。由一般 operator（總機）的工作內容可知此處所指的是分機號碼，故選 B。registration number為「牌照號碼」；stock number 指「庫存品編號」；serial number 為「產品序號或編號」。

答案	題目中譯	解題攻略
52. **(A)**	路易斯先生接管公司後的第一件事就是進行徹底地組織改造。 **(A) 接管** (B) 欺騙 (C) 相信 (D) 退出	此題在考片語。依文意可知此處是在表示「接管公司」，故選 A。
53. **(C)**	會議上所有的提議都會被紀錄在會議記錄裡。 (A) 提起 (B) 提起 **(C) 提起** (D) 提起	此句主要考關係代名詞的文法觀念。此句的主詞為 Any ideas that are brought up...（任何被提出的意見……），關係代名詞＋be動詞通常可一同省略（不可只省略關係代名詞），故正解為 C。
54. **(A)**	根據契約，你必須賠償我們的損失。 **(A) 賠償** (B) 消耗 (C) 遭遇 (D) 定義	此題是考字彙。compensate for...表示「賠償……」，故正解為 A。
55. **(B)**	成為正式員工前，你會有三個月的試用期。 (A) 給 **(B) 給** (C) 給 (D) 給	此句在考被動語氣的文法觀念，be 動詞後需接過去分詞，故選 B。

答案	題目中譯	解題攻略
56. (A)	傑夫最近似乎在工作上有所懈怠,身為主管,你應該提醒他做好本分。 (A) 懈怠 (B) 跟上 (C) 孤注一擲 (D) 相信	此題在考片語。由 remind him of his own duty(提醒他份內職責)可知選項中以 A 最適當,故選 A。keep up with 表示「跟上」;put one's shirt on 意為「孤注一擲」;take stock in 指「相信」。
57. (B)	主管對他的工作績效給予十分負面的評價,所以他今年無法加薪。 (A) 不整齊的 (B) 負面的 (C) 悲觀的 (D) 直接的	由 didn't get a raise(未得到加薪)可推論理由應與「負面評價」有關,故選 B。表示正面評價則為 positive remark。
58. (C)	怕你忘記,先提醒你下午三點要開會。 (A) 通知 (B) 通知 (C) 提醒 (D) 警告	由 in case you forget(未免你忘記),可知此處動詞以 remind(提醒)最適當。
59. (A)	艾美請喪假期間,茱莉亞會來代班。 (A) 在……之上 (B) 為了 (C) 在……之中 (D) 在……之下	表示「正在放……假」的用法為 on ... leave,故選 A。

答案	題目中譯	解題攻略
60. **(B)**	我已經辭職了，不過在找到接替的人之前我還是會來辦公室。 (A) 儘管 **(B) 直到** (C) 只要 (D) 因此	此題在考各種連接詞的用法。依文意可知最適合的連接詞為until，故選 B。
61. **(B)**	整個團隊花了數週的時間準備這場新提案的展示會。 (A) 準備 **(B) 準備** (C) 準備 (D) 準備	此題考 spend 這個特殊動詞的用法。「花時間做某事」用法為 spend (time)+V-ing，故答案為 B。
62. **(C)**	顧客退回了瑕疵品並要求退款。 (A) 獎賞 (B) 檢查 **(C) 退款** (D) 報告	依文意可知顧客要求退款，正確字彙為 refund。
63. **(B)**	您可以寄電子郵件給我，我再轉寄給相關部門。如有需要他們會跟您聯絡。 (A) 或者 **(B) 如果** (C) 雖然 (D) 除非	此題考連接詞的用法。由文意可知此處需要一個表示條件句的假設語氣，故選 B。

❶ 單句填空題 ― 中譯 & 解析

答案	題目中譯	解題攻略
64. **(A)**	廠長召集部門內所有員工開臨時會議。 **(A) 召集** (B) 打開 (C) 組裝 (D) 收集	召集會議所用的動詞應為 convene。assemble 亦表示「召集」，但受詞應為「人」而非「事物」；gather 後面應接複數名詞，意指「將……集合起來」，亦不適用。故以 A 為正解。
65. **(B)**	在公司內遭受不平等待遇導致他辭職離開。 (A) 達成 **(B) 導致** (C) 產生 (D) 起因於	此題在考片語用法。lead to ...表示「導致、致使……」，以文意判斷是為正解，與 result in 同義。
66. **(A)**	顧客堅持我們應該賠償他的損失。 **(A) 堅持** (B) 組成 (C) 抗拒 (D) 協助	此題在考字彙，根據文意可知insist 最為適合。
67. **(B)**	員工對新規定會激烈反對是可預期的。 (A) 不可靠的 **(B) 可預期的** (C) 規定的 (D) 可丟棄的	此題在考字彙，根據文意判斷 expectable 應為最適當的形容詞。

答案	題目中譯	解題攻略
68. **(D)**	我兩週前寫了一封信給你們的顧客中心抱怨關於產品的事情，但目前為止尚未得到任何回應。 (A) 回音 (B) 動作 (C) 答案 **(D) 回饋、回應**	answer 通常用來表示「回電」或「應門」；表示回信可用 reply 或 feedback，故此題選 D。
69. **(C)**	想參加今年國際通信電子展的公司行號請注意報名截止日期是九月十五日。 (A) 期間 (B) 時期 **(C) 截止日** (D) 長度	此處在表示申請的截止日期，故選 C。
70 **(B)**	勞工聯盟的發言人主張所有勞工都應得到合理的待遇以慰勞工作上的辛勞。 (A) 鑒於；根據 **(B) 作為……的報酬** (C) 因缺乏…… (D) 不管	此題在考片語。根據文意可知以 in reward for（做為……報酬）為最適當的解釋。in the light of 表示「鑒於；根據」；for want of 表示「因缺乏……而……」；regardless of 則為「不管」之意。

❶ 單句填空題 — 中譯＆解析

答案	題目中譯	解題攻略
71. (A)	求職者緊張到用發抖的聲音回答面試官的問題。 **(A) 申請人** (B) 供應者 (C) 主管 (D) 部屬	由 interviewer（面試官）這個字可推知主詞應為被面試者，選項中最適者為 A。
72. (B)	傳言銷售部部長將跳槽到 CBU，這個傳言已傳遍了整個辦公室。 (A) 退休 **(B) 跳槽** (C) 辭職 (D) 解雇	選項 A、C 中的動詞 retire 及 resign 後面的介系詞皆為 from，故可先刪去不考慮。job-hop to … 表示「跳槽至某處」，故為正解。
73. (A)	一般而言，我們產品的售價會比標價低兩成。 **(A) 較低** (B) 較小 (C) 較短 (D) 較小	表示低價時，形容詞為 low。此處需要比較級，故選 A。
74. (B)	歸功於銷售部的市場策略，新產品透過免費贈品成功地達到宣傳效果。 (A) 詭計 **(B) 策略** (C) 達成 (D) 練習	marketing strategy 表示「行銷策略」，故選 B。

答案	題目中譯	解題攻略
75. **(B)**	很抱歉，未經許可任何人不得進入發電室。 (A) 命令 **(B) 許可** (C) 注意 (D) 補貼	此題考字彙。without permission 表示「沒有許可的情況下」。動詞 allow 意指允許，但其名詞 allowance 卻為「津貼、零用金」之意。此處應選 B。
76. **(A)**	根據火車時刻表，下一班開往台北的車將在下午三點零六分發車。 **(A) 開往** (B) 灌輸、壓入 (C) 追逐 (D) 致力於	此題考片語用法。be bound for...表示「（交通工具）開往某地」，因此選 A。
77. **(B)**	工程師的過勞死顯示有很多公司強迫他們的員工超時工作。 (A) 地震 **(B) 過勞** (C) 癌症 (D) 憂鬱	由句尾 work overtime（加班工作）可知工程師的死因應與加班工作有關，故以 overwork 為最適當的解釋。death from overwork 指「過勞死」。
78. **(C)**	合約必須雙方同時簽署方能生效。 (A) 有效率的 (B) 傳染的 **(C) 有效的** (D) 感情的	此題在考字彙，注意勿為拼法相似的單字所混淆。根據文意可知形容詞應選 C。

❶ 單句填空題——中譯&解析

答案	題目中譯	解題攻略
79. **(A)**	抱歉，我們執行長目前沒空，而且我也無法提供他的連絡方式給您。 **(A) 有空的** (B) 可附上的 (C) 可接受的 (D) 可取得的	not available 通常為表示「某人沒空」或是「目前無法提供某物」的用法。根據文意此處應選 A。
80. **(A)**	辦公室雖無特定的著裝規定，但我確信迷你裙與熱褲並不適合穿來上班。 **(A) 適合的** (B) 公平的 (C) 足夠的 (D) 適宜的	此題在考字彙。根據文意此處乃在表示「不適合穿來上班」，故選 A。

Chapter

② 短文閱讀克漏字

中譯 & 解析

📝 短文閱讀 1：書信

親愛的布魯克斯先生，

寫這封信是想告訴您 ＿＿＿＿＿ 禮拜四的約會我將無法赴約。公司從

1. **(A) 預定的 scheduled**
   (B) 依序的 ordered
   (C) 批准 approval
   (D) 承諾 commitment

> 此句在表示「無法如同原定計畫見面」，as schedule 表示「如期」之意，故選 A。

禮拜二到週末之間有一個行銷活動，而我 ＿＿＿＿＿ 為負責人。

2. (A) 要求 asked
   (B) 認命 nominated
   (C) 被允許的 permitted
   (D) 規定的 given

> 此句在表示「被任命做某事」，to be nominated as … 為「受任命為……」之意，故選 B。

所以接下來的一整個禮拜我都不會在公司。我知道您的生意急需其他的銷售員幫忙，所以我建議您跟我們的區域經理雷恩布林

＿＿＿＿＿ 。

3. (A) 聯絡 contacted
   (B) 聯絡 contacting
   (C) 聯絡 be contacted
   (D) 聯絡 contact

> suggest 這個動詞的用法為「suggest that 人 should V」，而 that 與 should 可省略，故此處應選原形動詞，答案為 D。

他會幫你 ＿＿＿＿＿ 另一位銷售員。

4. (A) 編造 make up

   (B) 安排 set up

   (C) 觀望 look on

   (D) 結束 end up

> 由於他不能與Breaux 先生碰面，所以事先安排其他人來負責，故選 B。

他的電子郵件是 ryanblinn_south@tbc.com.tw 還有電話號碼是 0988123456。

這次沒能為您服務，請接受我誠摯的 ＿＿＿＿＿ 。

5. (A) 道歉 apologize

   (B) 道歉 apology

   (C) 難過 sorry

   (D) 遺憾的 regretful

> 接在形容詞 sincere 之後，可知此處應為名詞，選項中只有 B 符合，故選 B。

希望不久的將來能有機會幫忙您的生意。

誠摯此致，

黛咪‧黃

❷ 短文閱讀克漏字 —— 中譯＆解析

📝 短文閱讀 2：退貨處理

中譯 ＆ 解析

收信人： 王山繆先生
寄信人： C.N.B. 退貨處理中心
主旨： 關於您退回瑕疵品的要求

親愛的王先生，
我們獲悉您要求退回有瑕疵的商品。 在 ＿＿＿＿＿ 做處理之前，我

1. **(A) 繼續進行 proceed with**
   (B) 處理 deal with
   (C) 保持 keep up
   (D) 阻止 hold back

> 此處乃表示「繼續做某事」，若要以 keep up 來表示，則需
> 要介系詞 with 。因此以 A 為正解。

們想讓您知道對於這次交易您可以選擇更換 ＿＿＿＿＿ 商品或者退款。

2. (A) 易碎的 fragile
   (B) 指定的 specified
   (C) 不完美的 defective
   (D) 無效的 ineffective

> 此處在表示「瑕疵品」，故正確的形容詞應為 C。

如果您想 _____ 商品，我們會寄給您一個新品，當然運費是由我

3. (A) 債務 debt

   (B) 環境 environment

   (C) 收據 receipt

   (D) 更換 replacement

> 空格後提到we will send you a new item，推知應該要「更換」商品，因此答案選 D。

們這邊支出。如果您想退款，請提供我們原始購買 _____ 和貨運

4. (A) 證據 proof

   (B) 證人 witness

   (C) 證據 evidence

   (D) 收據 receipt

> 此處在表示「購買收據」，故以 D 為最適當的解答。

單。無論您做何選擇，請記得將瑕疵商品附同相關文件寄回給我
們。 我們由衷地為造成不便感到抱歉。 _____ 還有任何問題，

5. (A) 雖然 although

   (B) 也許 perhaps

   (C) 必須 must

   (D) 萬一 should

> should 當助動詞時，乃為「應該」之意，放在句首則表示「萬一」的句型，依文意此題正解為 D。

請儘管跟我們連絡。

📝 短文閱讀 3：飛行中廣播

中譯＆解析

早安，各位先生女士。我是你們的機長。歡迎搭乘東南航空168航班。我們目前以四百英里的時速航行於 ＿＿＿＿＿ 三萬英尺的高空中。

1. (A) 態度 attitude
   (B) 海拔 altitude
   (C) 代替 substitute
   (D) 緯度 latitude

> 此處乃在表示「所在位置的高度」，故以 B 為正解。這題在考相似字，因此對單字拼法不熟的考生可能會犯錯。

現在的時間是早上八點十五分。東京的 ＿＿＿＿＿ 晴朗無雲。

2. (A) 溫度 temperature
   (B) 氣候 weather
   (C) 風景 scenery
   (D) 娛樂 entertainment

> 空格後提到 clear and sunny（晴朗），推知和「天氣」有關，因此答案選 B。

我們 ＿＿＿＿＿ 將提早約十分鐘降落於成田機場。

3. (A) 相信 believing
   (B) 決定 deciding
   (C) 預期 expecting
   (D) 尋找 finding

此處在表示對「未來的預期」，因此用 expect 這個字。由於是「近期內確定發生的事情」，時態上習慣以「現在進行式」取代「未來式」。

約十五分鐘後座艙 ＿＿＿＿＿ 將會為您

4. (A) 員工 employees

    (B) 工人 workers

    (C) 飛機上的工作人員 crew

    (D) 淑女 ladies

此處在表示「飛機上的工作人員」，一般會以 crew 來表示，而不說 employee 或 worker。故正解為 C。

＿＿＿＿＿ 飲料。請坐回座位，放鬆心情並享受接下來的航程。

5. **(A) 提供 offer**

    (B) 交給 hand

    (C) 展示 show

    (D) 供應 supply

supply 通常用來表示「物資上的大量供給」，並不適用於表示機艙內的飲食供應，因此 offer 會比 supply 顯得適當，故選 A。

感謝您的合作。東亞航空祝您旅途愉快。

📝 短文閱讀 4：信用卡優惠介紹

中譯＆解析

如果要出外旅行，您需要搭配一張可彈性靈活運用的信用卡。CTB 尊榮卡，一張全球享惠的在地卡，在全世界有超過一萬五千個據點 _____ 刷卡，

1. (A) 將接受will accept

   (B) 被接受is accepted

   (C) 正接受is accepting

   (D) 接受accepted

> 這張卡在全球15,000個據點「被接受刷卡」，故選 B。

並提供下列 _____ ：

2. (A) 評論 comments

   (B) 編輯者 compilers

   (C) 好處 advantages

   (D) 投資 investments

> 空格後列出幾點CTB信用卡的優點，推知答案和此相關，因此答案選 C。

• 當地同等級產品中的最佳優惠方案，讓您 _____ 購物、用

3. **(A) 享權利entitles**

   (B) 使能夠enables

   (C) 准許allows

   (D) 准許permits

> 這題考動詞的用法。entitle someone to... 表示「享……權利」。其他選項動詞後面必須接不定詞，故不適用於此。

餐、娛樂以及旅行世界各地時的最佳優惠。

美金兩千元的緊急現金預支額度以及 _____ 或遺失時的隔日換卡

4. (A) 小偷thief

   (B) 被偷stolen

   (C) 偷竊theft

   (D) 偷竊stealing

> 由於 loss 為名詞，可知對等連接詞 or 前應同為一名詞，故選 C。

服務。

- 提供附有全套緊急協助與支援的 _____ 卡給您或您的小孩，

5. (A) 附件attachment

   (B) 額外的added

   (C) 補充的supplementary

   (D) 附件accessory

> supplementary credit card 指信用卡附卡，故選 C。

而且卡片額度由您來掌控。

📝 短文閱讀 5：起飛廣播

| 中譯＆解析 |

各位先生女士，歡迎搭乘由上海飛往倫敦的EI385航班。我們目前在第三跑道準備起飛且預計約五分鐘內開始 ＿＿＿＿＿＿ 。

1. **(A) 在空中in the air**
   (B) 飛行中的in-flight
   (C) 廣播的on-air
   (D) 上傳uploaded

> 由前文得知目前正等候起飛，可知此處要表示「起飛」，in the air表示「在空中」，故選 A。in-flight 表示「在飛行中」；on-air 表示「廣播中」；uploaded 表示「上傳」。

我們 ＿＿＿＿＿＿ 您繫好安全帶並妥善安置您座位下方或上方置物箱內的所有

2. (A) 假設suppose
   (B) 確保assure
   (C) 要求request
   (D) 使用apply

> 此處在表示「請您繫上安全帶……」，表示「請求」的動詞應為 C。

行李。 同時也請您確認 ＿＿＿＿＿＿ 您的座椅以及托盤桌已立起以便

3. (A) for
   (B) where
   (C) which
   (D) that

> make sure後的that+子句，習慣上用現在式表示要確保現在要做的事情，因此答案選 D。

飛機起飛。請關閉所有個人電子 _____ ，包含手提電腦與手機。

4. (A) 補給supplies

   (B) 裝置devices

   (C) 工具implements

   (D) 大型機器machinery

> 此處表示「電子儀器、用品、裝置」，表示「裝置」的名詞應為 B。

飛航期間 _____ 吸菸。

5. (A) 有限的limited

   (B) 控制controlled

   (C) 禁止prohibited

   (D) 可避免的avoidable

> 這句表示「航行中禁止吸煙」，表示「禁止」的字彙應選 C。

感謝您的合作。東亞航空祝您旅途愉快。

📝 短文閱讀 6：違反合約

中譯＆解析

2010年八月十五日

羅勃狄恩
台北市信義區信義路308號
電話：56042209#55
傳真：56042200
電子郵件：robertdean@utech.org.tw
網址：www.u-tech.sh.org.tw

致 尼爾森瓊斯，
很遺憾地通知您，您 ＿＿＿＿ 了2009年四月十日與我們所簽訂的協

1. (A) 在……控制下in the control of
   (B) 違反in breach of
   (C) 受……保護under the flag of
   (D) 為了in behalf of

> 這題在考片語用法。in breach of contract 表示「違反合約」
> 之意。其他片語皆不適用於此。故選 B。

議。在協議中您清楚地承諾自己會在新的智慧型觸控手機 ＿＿＿＿＿

2. **(A) 上市launch**
   (B) 公開disclosure
   (C) 揭露revelation
   (D) 促銷marketing

> 此處在表示「直至上市之後」，故選 A。

前針對所有技術層面的細節 _____ 密。您上週所發表的言論不只

3. (A) 保持maintaining

(B) 保持to maintain

(C) 保持to maintaining

(D) 保持 that maintaining

> 這題在考 commit 這個動詞的用法。commit oneself to N/V-ing 表示「對某事做出承諾」，可知此處應應選 to+V-ing，故選 C。

違反合約， _____ 含有可能不利於我們產品上市的負面評論。請

4. **(A) but 但是**

(B) or 或

(C) also 也

(D) and 並且

> not only A but (also) B 是指「不僅僅是A……，B也……」，also可以省略，因此答案選 A。

注意若在2010年八月底之前 _____ 正式且公開的撤銷言論，我們

5. (A) 將被做出

(B) 做出

(C) 已被做出

(D) 被做出

> 此處應為一被動語態，表示「除非正式公開的撤銷言論……」；連接詞 unless 前後的時態需一致，且 unless 之後的時態要以現在簡單式取代未來式，故選 D。

在別無選擇的情況下將採取法律行動。

誠摯此致，

羅勃狄恩

Chapter 3 長文閱讀測驗

中譯 & 解析

中譯

客戶支援分析師（約聘）

職責

★ 透過電話、電子郵件或傳真提供技術上的協助。

★ 提供第一級與第二級的支援以及故障排除。

★ 將問題登錄在服務平台資料庫。

★ 提供電腦端之間的問題管理。

★ 確保工作能力的持續進步。

★ 需繳交平台的日、週、月報給小組領導人。

★ 管理資料庫平台。

資格

★ 應徵者需至少有一個資訊工程相關文憑或學位。

★ 一到兩年相關領域的工作經驗。

★ 必備技能：微軟Microsoft Window OS、基礎網路、
Window XP、Microsoft Outlook 2011及Remote Access
troubleshooting

★ 能說英日中三國語言。

★ 有良好的溝通與人際關係技巧。

★ 應徵者會被派駐在日本東京。

★ 應徵者須為中華民國公民。

解析

答案	題目中譯	解題攻略
1. **(C)**	這則廣告的目的為何？ (A) 鼓勵員工去上電腦課。 (B) 要求員工盡忠職守。 **(C) 招募約聘的客戶支援分析師。** (D) 要求其員工改善對客戶的服務。	依內容可知此乃一則求才廣告，故以 C 為正解。在職稱前面加上 contract，則表示此為「約聘性質的、契約制」的職務。
2. **(A)**	根據這一則廣告，應徵這個職位的人應該是 **(A) 能講三種語言。** (B) 日本人。 (C) 小於三十五歲。 (D) 可以馬上到職。	由內文的必要條件中要求應徵者必須會說中英日三種語言，故可知答案為 A。其他選項內容皆與廣告不符。
3. **(C)**	下列何者不是客戶服務分析師的職責？ (A) 提供使用者技術方面的協助。 (B) 繳交日報給小隊長。 **(C) 有良好的人際關係技能。** (D) 管理資料庫平台。	此題要選出「不在職務範圍內」的答案，依內文對職務的敘述，可知選項 C 並未在其中，故選 C。

答案	題目中譯	解題攻略
4. **(D)**	根據這則廣告，candidates與下列何字意義相近？ (A) 嫌疑犯。 (B) 雇主。 (C) 教授。 **(D) 應徵者。**	此題在問單字意義。 candidate是指「面試者」或「應徵者」，與之最接近的單字為applicant，故選 D。
5. **(B)**	根據這則廣告，下列敘述何者錯誤？ (A) 其中一項職責是透過電子郵件提供技術上的協助。 **(B) 相關領域的工作經驗並不需要。** (C) 如果想獲得此工作，應徵者需有良好的溝通與人際關係技巧。 (D) 應徵者需至少有一個資訊工程相關文憑或學位。	1-2 year(s) of working experience in related field. （一到兩年相關的工作經驗。）由此得知相關經驗是必須故答案 B 為錯誤答案。

📝 長文閱讀 2

中譯

轉機 / 過境程序

如果您要在香港國際機場轉機，請注意下列步驟。

持有續程登機證的乘客，請您：

★ 沿著標示的方向到離境樓層的登機門。

★ 通過安全檢測。

★ 確認您的登機門編號與時間，至少在飛機起飛的三十分鐘前到達您的登機門。

未持有續程登機證的乘客，請您：

★ 確認您航空公司櫃台的位置。

★ 沿著標示的方向到指定的航空公司櫃檯區E1、E2或W1辦理登機。

★ 沿著標示的方向到離境樓層的登機門。

★ 通過安全檢測。

★ 確認您的登機門編號與時間，至少在飛機起飛的三十分鐘前到達您的登機門。

答案	題目中譯	解題攻略
1. **(B)**	這份注意事項最可能在哪裡看到？ (A) 在異國情調的餐廳裡。 **(B) 在機場。** (C) 在旅館辦理登記入住的櫃檯。 (D) 在旅行社。	由此篇告示標題可知內容與「轉機程序」相關，可知此篇告示應最可能被張貼在機場，故選 B。
2. **(D)**	根據這份注意事項，乘客最晚應該甚麼時候到達他們的登機門？ (A) 起飛前兩小時。 (B) 飛機到站後一小時。 (C) 飛機抵達的半小時前。 **(D) 飛機起飛的半小時前。**	告示中明文表示 at least 30 minutes before departure time（離境前三十分鐘），departure time= take-off time，皆表示「飛機起飛時間」；30 minutes=half an hour，皆表示「半小時」，故 D 為正解。
3. **(A)**	根據這份注意事項，未持有續程登機證的乘客在前往離境樓層的登機門前應該要做甚麼？ **(A) 在航空公司櫃台辦理登機。** (B) 領取他們的行李。 (C) 跟空服員要一份新的登機證。 (D) 打電話向旅行社求助。	告示中明文表示未持有續程登機証的旅客應先至航空櫃檯辦理，故此題應選 A。

❸ 長文閱讀測驗 ─ 中譯 & 解析

答案	題目中譯	解題攻略
4. **(A)**	根據這份注意事項，下列哪個選項並未提及？ **(A) 行李重量限制。** (B) 沿著標示的方向到離境樓層的登機門。 (C) 如果乘客未持有續程登機證，沿著標示的方向到指定的航空公司櫃檯區E1、E2或W1辦理登機。 (D) 登機時間。	根據注意事項，並未提到行李之事，因此可推論 A 為正確答案。
5. **(B)**	根據這份注意事項，procedure意義為何？ (A) 意外。 **(B) 程序。** (C) 節目。 (D) 發展。	由本文得知，是關於登機前的注意事項和步驟，因此可推論 B 為正確答案。

中譯

額外的假期 2023年12月22日和 2023年12月29日

2023年十月二十九日

親愛的工作同仁：

　　我知道你們很多人都已經開始規劃冬季的假期。過了一個忙碌的秋季大家都期待著與家人朋友相處的時間。 雖然辛勤的工作是TBS繁榮的基礎，大家仍須在工作與休閒間取得平衡才能繼續下去。

　　因此，我很高興地在此宣布公司今年除了原有的假日十二月二十四日，二十五日，以及一月一日之外，將讓全體員工再多休兩個禮拜五，包括十二月二十二日以及十二月二十九。這多出來的休假日將適用於所有符合福利資格的TBS同仁。 部分擔任必要差勤的員工仍須在十二月二十二日與二十九上班。主管們將會與這兩天需要來上班的同仁們聯繫，視情況決定是否要另外挑兩天休假或者直接領取相當的薪酬。感謝大家的配合與體諒。

　　希望這額外的休假能讓大家為即將到來的假日多增添一點樂趣。

此致，
瑪姬
Margarita S. Cliff
人事經理

解析

答案	題目中譯	解題攻略
1. **(B)**	這段宣布是想傳達甚麼訊息給同事們？ (A) 公司要裁掉一半的員工。 **(B) 公司要讓大家多放幾天假。** (C) 公司將與TBS合併。 (D) 公司要求所有員工聖誕節當天來上班。	根據內文可知本公告乃在傳遞「公司給予員工額外休假」之訊息，故答案為B。lay off 表示「裁員」；merge with...表示「與……合併」。
2. **(A)**	根據這段宣布，12/22和29要來上班的員工可以有甚麼選擇？ **(A) 領取相當的薪酬。** (B) 找別人代班。 (C) 請病假。 (D) 跟工會抱怨。	此題在問「無法於額外休假日休假的員工可做的選擇」，根據公告內文可知A為正解。hold the fort 表示「暫時代理」。
3. **(C)**	在第二段中，以下何者為不屬於符合福利資格的同仁？ (A) TBS的正式員工。 (B) 人事經理，瑪姬。 **(C) 臨時工。** (D) 辦公室助理。	benefits-eligible 乃表示「符合福利資格」之意，一般為正職或全職員工才具備此資格，選項中只有C 明顯為非正職員工，故選 C。day labor 指「臨時工」。

答案	題目中譯	解題攻略
4. **(D)**	看完這段公告，員工感受如何？ (A) 他們覺得受挫。 (B) 他們覺得擔心。 (C) 他們覺得可怕。 **(D) 他們覺得開心。**	由公告得知多了兩天休假，因此員工的感覺應該是正面的，故推知答案選D。
5. **(C)**	根據這公告，下列選項何者為真？ (A) 公告發布日期在12月25號以後。 (B) TBS公司將多給員工三天額外休假。 **(C) Maggie發布此項公告。** (D) 主管們在十二月29日都要上班。	四個選項中，選項(A)應該在12月25之前，選項(B)是兩天額外假期。選項(C)正確，選項(D)並沒硬性規定，故答案選 C。

📝 長文閱讀 4

中譯

美國失業率降到8.8%，創兩年新低

華盛頓－最新發表的2011年三月美國失業率百分之8.8，達兩年來新低。從1948到2010年期間，美國平均失業率為百分之5.7，1982年十一月的百分之10.8為歷史高點，1953年五月的百分之2.5為最低點。

「這與復甦逐漸出現動能的觀點非常吻合，因此經濟仍在持續復甦，這是非常好的消息，」位於紐約阿爾巴尼的休強森顧問公司的主任投資長，休強森這麼表示。

美國非農業就業人數在三月份增加了二十一萬六千人。專業與商業服務，健康看護，休閒，醫療與礦業的工作機會均增加。製造業的工作機會持續在成長。

三月份的新工作都來自於私人企業，繼二月所增加的二十四萬個工作機會，三月份又再增加了二十三萬個。政府提供的工作則少了一萬四千個，連續五個月遞減，地方政府也解雇了一萬五千名工人。

雖然能源價格的上漲侵蝕了消費者的信心，經濟學者並不認為就業市場會就此踩煞車。

答案	題目中譯	解題攻略
1. **(D)**	從這段新聞我們可知道什麼訊息？ (A) 美國正處於經濟萎縮。 (B) 消費者信心助長了能源價格上漲。 (C) 2011年三月份公共事業增加了一萬四千個工作機會。 **(D) 美國經濟似乎在復甦中。**	由內文可知美國經濟正在復甦，故以 D 為正解。其他選項皆與內文不符。
2. **(A)**	根據這段新聞，下列何者為真？ **(A) 美國地方政府在過去五個月共解雇了一萬五千名工人。** (B) 企業對於長期僱用全職員工仍持保留心態。 (C) 除了製造業，所有行業與專職的就業均成長。 (D) 企業較願意雇用短期工而非長期的正職員工。	此題要選符合內文的敘述。選項中除 A 之外，B、C、D 所述皆與內文不符，故選 A。declining a fifth straight month 表示「連續五個月減少……」；local governments let go 15,000 workers 表示「地方政府遣散15,000名員工」。

答案	題目中譯	解題攻略
3. **(C)**	根據這段新聞,下列哪一項結果侵蝕了消費者信心? (A) 更多的企業願意給予員工長期的保障。 (B) 政府的工作機會持續五個月衰退。 **(C) 雖然經濟在復甦,能源價格仍持續上漲。** (D) 企業將停止雇用全職員工。	此題在問腐蝕消費者信心的原因。根據文章內容可知原因為「能源價格的上揚」,故選 C。
4. **(B)**	根據這段新聞,第三段的片語trend up意思為何? (A) 減少。 **(B) 上漲。** (C) 允許。 (D) 改變。	trend有趨勢之意,trend up 的片語意思為上升趨勢,可由片語的前後文推知,故答案為 B。
5. **(C)**	根據這段新聞,為何企業較有意願去做這些長期的投資? (A) 因為他們不需要聘請更多的員工。 (B) 因為未來他們可以賺更多錢。 **(C) 因為比起幾個月前非常謹慎的心態,現在的企業已較有信心去接納長期工作的全職員工。** (D) 因為經濟學家給予良好建議。	由,最後一段提到:Employment gains have been modest in recent months, so in that sense I think businesses that were initially very wary of taking on permanent full-time employees are feeling more confident now than some months ago,故推知答案為 C。

中譯

> 親愛的珍妮佛 鮑小姐，
>
> 　　上週五2023年三月三十一日很高興跟你會面。
>
> 　　我們對於你出色的書本編輯背景以及在敦煌書局的資歷感到印象非常深刻。與我們總編討論過你的履歷之後，我很樂意提供您主編的職位，以及台幣四萬兩千元的月薪。關於福利的部分，你將享有全民健保以及勞工保險。如果你對這個職位有興趣，我們可再來討論更多的細節。
>
> 　　請仔細考慮這個工作機會，然後在四月八日禮拜五前給我回覆。
>
> 　　我們誠摯期待歡迎你加入我們團隊。
>
> 此致，
>
> *Andy Hsiao*
> 人力資源部經理

解析

答案	題目中譯	解題攻略
1. **(C)**	從這封信，我們可以知道關於珍妮佛鮑的部分為何？ (A) 她沒有書本編輯的相關工作經驗。 (B) 她今年剛從大學畢業。 **(C) 她上週有工作面試。** (D) 她決定不要這個工作機會。	根據信件內容可知此為 Jennifer Bao 的面試錄取通知。由信件開頭第一句便可知 Jennifer Bao 的面試時間為上週五，因此可知此題答案為 C。

答案	題目中譯	解題攻略
2. **(B)**	珍妮佛鮑最有可能申請的職位為？ (A) 總編。 **(B) 主編。** (C) 助理編輯。 (D) 人力資源部經理。	由信件中 offer you the position of editor-in-chief 可知 Jennifer Bao 所應徵的職務應為 editor-in-chief，故選B。
3. **(B)**	珍妮佛鮑最晚應該何時回覆？ (A) 2023年3月31日。 **(B) 2023年四月八日。** (C) 四月底。 (D) 2023年底。	此題在問 Jennifer Bao 最晚必須在何時回覆信件。由信件中 by the end of this Friday, April 8可知答案為B。
4. **(B)**	此封信的目的為何？ (A) 對工作提出正式抱怨。 **(B) 對面試者提出工作通知。** (C) 要求於四月八號前完成工作。 (D) 通知加薪一事。	由本封信提到面試，滿意背景和資歷，最後提到薪水和福利，故推知答案為B。
5. **(D)**	"outstanding" 與下列何字意義最相近？ (A) 複雜的。 (B) 恐怖的。 (C) 有趣的。 **(D) 傑出的。**	由We were very impressed. ，以及通知對方來面試，表示背景和資歷是很「傑出的」，故推知答案為 D。

中譯

雪爾頓 租車中心

姓名： 張博恩
護照號碼： *P1269573400*

租借城市，機場代碼或美國地區區碼
蘭開斯特機場
☑ 我將於其它地方的雪爾頓租車中心歸還這輛租用車。

歸還城市，機場代碼或美國地區區碼
愛倫鎮 *LVI* 機場

租車日期與時間：
2023年四月十三日上午十點

還車日期與時間：
2023年五月三日下午兩點

租用車款：
全尺寸/標準型：
車輛有四個門，可乘坐四到五人，可放置四到五個行李箱（行李容量隨行李大小與車型而異）。

□ 我可享折扣 （CDP, PC, 折價券或其他）

答案	題目中譯	解題攻略
1. **(A)**	這份文件的主要用途為？ **(A) 預訂租車。** (B) 取消餐廳訂位。 (C) 機票確認。 (D) 預約牙醫。	由本表格抬頭的 car rental 可知此乃一張租車申請的表格，故選 A。
2. **(D)**	從這份文件中可以知道關於張博恩的事為？ (A) 他2023年四月十三日會在愛倫鎮 L V I 機場。 (B) 他想在藍斯開特租一間公寓。 (C) 他將會在租車的同一地點還車。 **(D) 他租車未享折扣。**	由申請表可看出 I have a discount. 欄並未被勾選，可知 Chang Bo En 並無享有租車優惠的條件，故選 D。
3. **(A)**	張博恩租車的時間為多久？ **(A) 約三週。** (B) 約一週。 (C) 四小時。 (D) 沒提到。	此題在問 Chang Bo En 需要用車的時間。由申請表中的取車日與還車日可知 Chang Bo En 需要車子的時間約為三周，故選 A。
4. **(A)**	張博恩會在哪裡歸還汽車？ (A) 碼愛倫鎮 L V I 機場。 (B) 雪梨。 **(C) 紐約機場。** (D) 碼蘭開斯特機場	由此文件的資訊，歸還地點哪一欄可得知歸還地點為：Allentown L V I Airport，故推知答案為A。

答案	題目中譯	解題攻略
5. **(C)**	根據這份文件，下列選項何者為真？ (A) 租車種類為卡車。 (B) 張博恩將於四月13號還車。 **(C) 張博恩用護照租車。** (D) 車輛有兩個門，可放置兩個行李箱。	由文件可知租標準汽車，於四月13號租車，車輛可放四個行李箱以上。另外，文件中留下護照資訊，故推知答案為 C。

📝 長文閱讀 7

中譯

搬遷啟事

致我們重要的顧客與夥伴，

請注意我們辦公室將於2010年十月一日起遷移至下列地址
（原辦公室隔壁）

台北市大安區忠孝東路四段
288巷223號太子大樓十樓1033~1035號房
我們的電話與傳真號碼保持不變。

您誠摯的，
飛行者貨運有限公司。

答案	題目中譯	解題攻略
1. **(A)**	這份公告的主要目的為何？ **(A) 辦公室搬遷的通知。** (B) 暫停營業的公告。 (C) 重新營業的公告。 (D) 招募人員的廣告。	由此公告的標題可知此乃為一則「搬遷啟示」，故選 A。relocation 為「改變位置」之意。
2. **(C)**	根據這份公告，新辦公室何時啟用？ (A) 再過幾天。 (B) 就是今天。 **(C) 2010年十月初。** (D) 2010年十月某一天。	此題在問新辦公室何時啟用。由公告中 with effective from 1st October 可知時間為十月一日起，故選 C。英文中常以 this very day 強調「就是今天」。
3. **(D)**	照下列那一種做法，顧客或夥伴將無法與飛行者貨運有限公司取得連絡？ (A) 打飛行者貨運原來的電話號碼。 (B) 傳一封信給飛行者貨運原來的傳真號碼。 (C) 親自拜訪新地址。 **(D) 寄信到原地址。**	此題在問顧客以何種方式將無法連絡上 Flyer Shipping Ltd. 這間公司。由公告內容可知公司除變更地點之外，電話與傳真都沒變，故可知無法取得連絡的方法為選項D。

答案	題目中譯	解題攻略
4. **(B)**	根據這份公告，下列選項何者為真？ (A) 辦公室將搬離舊址很遠之處。 **(B) 電話維持不變。** (C) 辦公室將於九月重新營業。 (D) 太子大樓沒有電梯。	(A) 錯誤，搬到隔壁。 (B) 正確。 (C) 錯誤，於十月1號。 (D) 錯誤，位於十樓，推知有電梯。 故答案為 B。
5. **(B)**	根據這份公告，下列選項何者並未提及？ (A) 公司名稱。 **(B) 老闆姓名。** (C) 重新營業日期。 (D) 傳真號碼。	此份公告提到公司名稱，營業日期以及新辦公室的傳真號碼，並未提到公司老闆的姓名，故推知答案為 B。

📝 長文閱讀 8

中譯

> 　　勞委會不久前公布了一份調查結果，一位任職於紐約科技機構的二十九歲男子，常態性的加班工作，猝死的原因為過勞。
>
> 　　徐姓受害者，於2006年進入紐約開始當工程師且頻繁地超時工作。在他死亡的前半年，每個月的加班時數都達到八十個小時，有時甚至一個月長達139個小時。
>
> 　　當徐先生的雙親九月在記者會上控訴徐的死因為過勞時，這個案例首度引發了公眾的關注。他並沒有任何舊疾且正值壯

年，卻突然地死於心臟病或中風，這是典型的過勞死徵狀。官方一開始拒絕將此案例認定為過勞死，因為他們發現徐死於心源性休克，應與職業無關。然而，經官方重新評估這個案例後認為徐的死應歸類為過勞死，因為第二次的調查發現徐的猝死與他的長期超時工作有強烈的關聯。

立委與勞工運動者長期指控勞委會對危險的工作環境視而不見且在現今的系統之下，過勞死想要得到合理的補償幾乎是不可能的事。

勞工保險局將接手此案例，且可能會補償工作者的家庭約當四十五個月的薪資。

解析

答案	題目中譯	解題攻略
1. **(C)**	根據這篇文章，這位二十九歲工程師的死因為？ (A) 先天性心臟病。 (B) 吸毒過量。 **(C) 長期超時工作。** (D) 酒精中毒。	此題在問工程師的死因。依文章內容可知答案為 C。
2. **(A)**	根據這篇文章，過勞死的典型徵狀為何？ **(A) 心臟病或中風猝死。** (B) 長期憂鬱症或恐慌症。 (C) 長期失眠或疲勞。 (D) 呼吸窘迫而死。	此題在問過勞死的典型徵兆。依文章內容可知答案為 A。

答案	題目中譯	解題攻略
3. **(B)**	根據這篇文章,下列敘述何者為真? (A) 受害者的家庭不可能為他們兒子的過勞死得到任何補償。 **(B) 勞工保險局可能會給付四十五個月的薪資做為受害者死亡的補償。** (C) 當這件事引發公眾關注時,勞委會馬上將這位工程師的死亡歸類為過勞死。 (D) 勞工運動者對勞委會改善目前工作環境的努力感到滿意。	此題要選正確敘述。由文章最後一段可知 B 為正解。其他選項內容皆與內文不符。
4. **(B)**	根據這篇文章,第四段 occupation這個單字,與下列何字意義相近? (A) 交通。 **(B) 工作。** (C) 投資。 (D) 背景。	文章提到:the second investigation showed that Hsu's sudden death was strongly correlated with his long- term working overtime,由working overtime(超時工作),推知答案和工作有關,故選 B。

答案	題目中譯	解題攻略

5.
(B)

如果勞工保險局將接手此案例，可能會補償工作者的家庭多少錢呢？

(A) 約一年薪資。
(B) 約45個月的薪資。
(C) 至少十萬元。
(D) 本文未提及。

由文章最後一段提到：The Bureau of Labor Insurance is likely to compensate the worker's family the equivalent of 45 months' salary.（勞工保險局可能會補償工作者的家庭約當四十五個月的薪資。），故推知答案為 B。

📝 長文閱讀 9

中譯

2011年三月十五日

失物招領公告

　　總務處辦公室有一些從辦公室大樓各處發現的各式物品。這些東西如下：鑰匙、手機、iPods、數位相機、CD、隨身聽、耳環、錢、皮夾、手錶和一些雜物。

　　如果你有這類的遺失物品且可以正確識別出來，請聯絡總務處處長唐大衛，分機號碼8308。

　　所有物品只保留十四天，逾期將立即予以拍賣或捐贈給慈善機構。

答案	題目中譯	解題攻略
1. **(A)**	根據這一份公告,物主須在何時領取他們的失物? **(A) 2011年三月二十八日之前。** (B) 2011年三月十五日之前。 (C) 週末之前。 (D) 三月底之前。	此題要問失物所有人應在何時認領失物。由告示中 All items not claimed within 14 days, following the date of this listing… 可知認領期限為公告日起14天內。因此由3月15日起算起14天,可得到答案為 A。
2. **(C)**	根據這一份公告,物主須到哪裡領取他們的失物? (A) 警察局。 (B) 警衛室。 **(C) 總務處辦公室。** (D) 接待室。	此題在問失物招領處的地點。由告示內容可之失物招領的地點為 the Office of General Affairs,故選 C。
3. **(B)**	根據這一份公告,未領取的失物將會如何處理? (A) 燒毀。 **(B) 拍賣。** (C) 賣給慈善機構。 (D) 當垃圾丟棄。	此題在問未被認領的失物的處置方式。由告示最後一句 will be put up to auction(交付拍賣)或「捐給慈善機構」,故可知答案為 B。

❸ 長文閱讀測驗 ── 中譯 & 解析

答案	題目中譯	解題攻略
4. **(A)**	在第一段中，miscellaneous與下列何字意義相近？ **(A) 各式各樣的。** (B) 分類的。 (C) 收集的。 (D) 隨機的。	miscellaneous 意指「各種各樣的」，與之意義最相近的為 assorted。
5. **(C)**	根據這一份公告，下列敘述何者為非？ (A) 失物招領於三月貼出公告。 (B) 如果你有遺失物品，請聯絡總務處處長，分機號碼8308。 **(C) 所有物品只保留十天。** (D) 這些遺失物包含數位相機。	由公告可知所有物品可以保留十四天，故推知選項(C)為錯誤。

📝 長文閱讀 10

中譯

寄信人： 丹尼爾華森先生，
    Daisy & Daniel's負責人
收件人： 湯瑪斯羅德曼先生
日期： 2011-04-12
主題： 商業活動邀請

親愛的羅德曼先生，

　　希望您收到信時身體與精神都處於最佳狀態。您是我們尊貴的客戶之一，我們想要感謝您的光顧並藉此機會邀請您參加我們的新裝系列發表會，2011年五月十日下午五點在麗晶飯店。

　　我們準備了開幕式與晚餐派對以感謝我們的顧客。我們想介紹我們新的時裝系列給我們尊貴的代理商與顧客，所以希望所有人都能參加這個派對。

　　請於2011年四月三十日前與我們確認。
　　由衷盼望您的蒞臨。

您誠摯的，
丹尼爾華森

寄信人： 湯瑪斯羅德曼先生
收件人： 丹尼爾華森先生，
主題：回覆： 商業活動邀請

親愛的丹尼爾，

　　感謝您善意的邀請。不巧地，您舉辦活動當天我已有其他約會，我恐怕沒辦法參加您的開幕式。

　　請接受我誠摯的向您祝賀新時裝系列的發表。
　　希望慶祝會後我們可以另外約個時間聚聚。

您的，
湯瑪斯羅德曼

❸ 長文閱讀測驗—中譯＆解析

解析

答案	題目中譯	解題攻略
1. **(B)**	從這些信裡我們可以得知什麼訊息？ (A) 羅德曼先生受邀到華森先生的結婚典禮。 **(B) 羅德曼先生拒絕了邀請，因為已先跟別人約好。** (C) 麗晶飯店會有記者會。 (D) 羅德曼先生將親自參加開幕式。	第一封郵件旨在邀請對方出席新產品發表會，而第二封郵件則婉拒邀請。觀兩封郵件內文可知 B 為正解。
2. **(A)**	信最有可能是下列那一個日期寄出的？ **(A) 2011年四月二十八日。** (B) 2011年五月十日。 (C) 2011年五月二十八日。 (D) 2011年四月十日。	此題在問回覆的郵件最可能在哪一天寄出。由於第一封郵件要求對方於 30th of April, 2011 之前回覆，因此可推論 A 為最有可能的日期。
3. **(D)**	根據這些電子郵件，羅德曼先生與華森先生之間的關係是？ (A) 他們是雇主與員工。 (B) 他們是家族老友。 (C) 他們是遠親。 **(D) 他們有生意往來。**	此題在問邀請者與受邀者的關係。由第一封郵件中的 thank you for your business，可知兩造有生意上的往來，故選項中以 D 最適當。

答案	題目中譯	解題攻略
4. **(A)**	羅德曼先生受邀的場合為下列何者？ **(A) 新產品發表會。** (B) 歲末派對。 (C) 大學研討會。 (D) 訂婚典禮。	此題在問羅德曼先生受邀參加的場合為何。由第一封郵件可知他是受邀參加一場新產品發表會，故選A。
5. **(C)**	下列敘述何者無法從信中推論出來？ (A) 湯瑪斯羅德曼在Daisy & Daniel's 新裝系列發表會的同一天有事。 (B) 湯瑪斯羅德曼希望跟華森先生在開幕式後可以約個時間聚聚。 **(C) 湯瑪斯羅德曼將派他的助理經理威爾先生代表他出席，因為他無法親自到場。** (D) Daisy & Daniel's 是一間從事時裝生意的公司。	此題要選無法從兩封郵件內容得知的訊息。受邀者回信中婉拒出席，並未說明會委任其他人代替他出席，故應選 C。

中譯

本報記者張保羅

　　勞委會正在考慮修改颱風行政準則。勞委會表示截至目前為止較傾向於要求雇主不能拒絕支薪給放「颱風假」的員工，且如果員工於期間仍須出勤，雇主須多支付額外的薪資。不過，這項政策尚未定案。

　　根據目前的法規，如當地方政府宣布因颱風放假一天，該項宣布只適用於政府機關員工與學校。私人企業的員工是否能放颱風假須視其聘僱合約的規定。即使雇主讓員工放假，他們也不需給付正常的薪資。

　　勞工團體去年起就跟勞委會請願，要求遇上颱風假時，一般勞工應與人民公僕享有同等的待遇。因此，勞委會為此正在研擬新的準則，且表示今年颱風季節開始前他們就會嘗試宣布新的颱風行政準則。草稿中提到，當工作地、居住地或上下班往返之區域的地方政府一旦宣布放颱風假，勞工就可以跟著放假，且缺席不應視為曠職或私人事假。雇主不能要求員工補上班，不能拒付出席津貼或藉故開除。

　　可預見的，雇主們仍會嘗試在新準則裡找漏洞，並要求勞工在颱風假上班。然而準則的制訂並沒有法律基礎，無法對違反準則的雇主們罰款。政府只能「鼓勵」雇主遵守行政準則。

　　至於員工放颱風假可支薪，目前仍在勞資雙方代表的激烈辯論之中。

2009年七月三日

親愛的全體同仁：

　　這封信是用來通知GMC的全體員工，大家必須在2009年七月十八日禮拜六那一天來上班，以彌補2009年六月二十三日禮拜一颱風假的缺席。

　　任何一位2009年七月十八日無法來上班的人，必須事先跟主管請假，且必須從你七月份的薪水扣除一天的薪資。

　　如果有任何疑問，請直接找我或任何人事部的同仁。

誠摯的問候
辛蒂布魯克
人事部經理

解析

答案	題目中譯	解題攻略
1. **(D)**	根據這則新聞和電子郵件，下列敘述何者正確？ (A) GMC 要求員工颱風假期間來上班。 (B) GMC 想要把放颱風假當成員工曠職。 (C) 雇主依法須強制給與員工颱風假並支付正常薪資。 **(D) GMC 是私人機構而不是政府單位。**	此題要選正確的描述。由公告郵件比照新聞內容可知此GMC 應為一家私人企業而非政府機構，故選D。

答案	題目中譯	解題攻略
2. **(D)**	我們可以從這則新聞和電子郵件推論出？ (A) 如果GMC不讓員工放颱風假，他們會被罰款。 (B) 很明顯地GMC嘗試在鑽新颱風準則的漏洞。 (C) 如果要員工在颱風假期間來上班，雇主應給予員工額外津貼。 **(D) GMC變相強迫員工為颱風假的缺席補上一天班。**	由公告郵件內容可知GMC 要求無法補班的員工必須請事假，且將扣除一天薪資，可知此乃變相強迫員工補班之行為，故選 D。
3. **(C)**	勞工團體向勞委會請願何事？ (A) 他們要求雇主拿回給放颱風假員工的薪資。 (B) 他們要求新的颱風假政策要有法律效力。 **(C) 他們要求遇上颱風假時一般勞工應與公務員享有同等的待遇。** (D) 他們堅持勞委會要在颱風季節來臨前將新颱風假政策定案。	此題在問勞工團體向勞工局作何請願。由文章內容可知C 為正解。選項 A中，hold back wages 表示「不發放薪資」並不符合團體的訴求，故該選項並非正解。

答案	題目中譯	解題攻略
4. **(B)**	在甚麼情況下，GMC的員工應事先請假？ (A) 當他們病得太嚴重而不能在颱風假期間來上班。 **(B) 當他們無法為颱風假補班來上班時。** (C) 當地方政府宣布因颱風放假一天時。 (D) 當他們對新颱風行政準則或規定有疑問時。	此題在問 GMC 員工在何種情形下應事先請事假。依內文可知 B 為正解。
5. **(A)**	這封電子郵件的主要用意為？ **(A) 為了通知員工颱風假補班日期。** (B) 為了支持新颱風行政準則在今年的颱風季節前公佈。 (C) 為了反對如何支付放颱風假的員工薪資的現行規定。 (D) 為了鼓勵雇主依循勞委會最新的颱風假政策。	此題在問這封電子郵件的主旨。由郵件內容知道其旨在通知員工颱風假補班的日期，故選 A。

中譯

派崔克賴，
白金股份有限公司的高科技部長

****

收件人： 派崔克賴，白金股份有限公司的高科技部長

親愛的賴先生，

　　很抱歉通知你白金公司原訂六月八到十日舉辦的2011年度研討會因一些內部因素將延遲到六月十五到十七日。研討會計畫將在台北信義區亞太會館的第三會議廳舉行。你可在附檔內找到最新的研討會時程。

　　此外，六月十二日在我們辦公室大樓的會議室將會有會前會。請撥空參加。

　　延遲若造成你任何的不便，請接受我們誠心的道歉。
非常感謝你的體諒。

您忠實的，
愛蜜麗

白金2011年度研討會時程表

第一天／2011年六月十五日星期三

14：00 – 16：30	報到－阿波羅廳，201會議室
16：30 – 17：30	代表簡介（強制參加）－阿波羅廳，201會議室
17：30 – 19：00	晚餐
19：00 – 21：00	開幕式
21：00 – 21：30	主管/指導員接待會

第二天／2011年六月十六日星期四

09：00 – 12：00	委員會議 I
12：00 – 13：30	午餐
13：30 – 16：30	委員會議II
16：30 – 17：30	主管會議
17：30 – 19：00	晚餐
19：00 – 22：00	白金派對

第三天／2011年六月十七日星期五

09：00 – 12：00	委員會議III
12：00 – 13：30	午餐
13：30 – 16：30	委員會議IV
16：30 – 17：00	最後主管會議
17：00 – 17：30	閉幕式與頒獎

（尚未定案）

解析

答案	題目中譯	解題攻略
1. **(C)**	這封電子郵件主要目的為？ (A) 公布新的員工守則。 (B) 取消既定的年度研討會。 **(C) 通知研討會延期。** (D) 跟處長改約會的時間。	由郵件內容中 conference scheduled on … will be procrastinated till…（原訂於……舉行之會議將延至……）可知其主旨乃在做年度會議延遲舉行的通知。故選 C。
2. **(D)**	派崔克賴預計在年度研討會前要去？ (A) 要求年度研討會最新的時程表。 (B) 回應研討會的邀請。 (C) 為研討會的延遲道歉。 **(D) 參加會前會。**	此題在問派崔克在年會之前應做之事。由郵件內容可知他被要求撥冗出席會前研討會，故選 D。
3. **(C)**	下列資訊何者不包含在附檔內？ (A) 研討會參加者的報到時間。 (B) 三天研討會的大略程序。 **(C) 出席研討會的參加人員列表。** (D) 年度研討會結束的確切時間。	此題要選出未出現在附加檔案內的資訊。由會議行程表中未詳列與會者名單，可知 C 為正解。

答案	題目中譯	解題攻略
4. **(A)**	從上面信中的時程表我們可以知道？ **(A) 研討會的參加人員可能是公司的主管。** (B) 研討會改期可能是因為天氣惡劣。 (C) 研討會是為了慶祝公司擴大經營。 (D) 參加者可以帶個人助理陪同。	此題要選出能從郵件及其附加檔案中所能得知之資訊。依行程表中活動主要為 committee session（委員會議）及 head delegate meeting（主管代表會議）可知最適合的選項應為 A。其他選項內容皆無法由所附資料推論出來。
5. **(C)**	根據上面的信與時程表，下列敘述何者有誤？ (A) 年度研討會將持續三天兩夜。 (B) 研討會包含四個委員會議。 **(C) 信上所附的時程表是最終版本。** (D) 舉辦研討會的地點保持不變。	此題要選出錯誤的敘述。由行程表最後出現的 still subject to change.（仍會作修改）可知這個行程安排並非定案版本，故選 C。

中譯

親愛的布朗先生，

　　回覆您三月二十一日的信，您問到參加台灣舉辦的2011年商業與人權國際研討會是否安全，我們很堅定地告訴您一點都不需要擔心。

　　我們知道您是擔心受到日本輻射影響，但根據原子能委員會表示，東京的輻射程度為安全的，何況是台灣。

　　台灣目前確實沒有輻射汙染。您可放鬆心情參加計畫的會議。我在信中附了一篇文章，希望能解除您的疑慮。

　　我們期待您四月十五日的光臨。

最好的問候，
蘇珊強森

來自日本的輻射塵不會造成危險

　　根據原子能委員會(AEC)表示，日本毀壞的核能電廠所釋放出的輻射塵將飄到台灣，其量不會對人體健康造成威脅。

　　根據氣象條件，來自日本的放射性沉澱物將在幾天內到達台灣預計輻射程度將遠低於可容許的上限每小時 0.2 維西佛，因此將不會對人體健康造成危險。

　　「不需對輻射外洩感到恐慌，因為量小到不會對人體健康有傷害。」AEC 輻射保護部李部長強調。他說日本輻射塵的輻射程

度約為照一次胸部 X 光片的三千分之一，所以我們無需擔心。

李也説自核能危機開始，721 項來自日本的食品檢測都沒有發現達危險等級的輻射物質。

他補充説 AEC 正計畫要增加空氣以及農產品和魚類的輻射物質檢測頻率，以強化台灣的輻射監控。

解析

答案	題目中譯	解題攻略
1. **(B)**	布朗先生來台灣最可能的目的為？ (A) 觀光。 **(B) 做生意。** (C) 探親。 (D) 渡假。	此題在問 Mr. Brown 訪台的主要目的。由郵件內容可知他是要來參與研討會，選項中以 B 最適當，故選 B。
2. **(D)**	這篇文章主要是在討論？ (A) 日本核能反應爐釋出的輻射塵將如何傷害人體健康。 (B) 如何避免被日本釋出的輻射塵影響。 (C) 輻射如何破壞日本鄰近國家的旅遊業。 **(D) 日本外洩的輻射量有多微小，因此不會對人體構成危害。**	此題在問文章主旨。由內容可知該文旨在説明來自日本的輻射外洩量幾乎不會危及健康，故選 D。

❸ 長文閱讀測驗—中譯 & 解析

答案	題目中譯	解題攻略
3. **(D)**	從這封信與文章我們可以知道？ (A) 目前所有來自日本的漁產品都被禁止。 (B) 商業與人權國際研討會將會延期。 (C) 來自日本核能反應爐的輻射塵將不會到台灣。 **(D) AEC 將會強化台灣的輻射監控。**	此題要選可從郵件及文章得到的訊息。除選項 D 之外，其他選項內容皆與內文不符，故選 D。
4. **(A)**	下列何者最能說明為什麼來台灣是安全的？ **(A) 來自日本的放射性沉澱物輻射程度將遠低於可容許的上限。** (B) 全部721項進口自日本的食物自日本核能危機後都將做檢測。 (C) 空氣中以及農漁產品都沒發現含有輻射物質。 (D) 檢測空氣中輻射物質的頻率將會增加。	此題要選為何來台灣是安全無虞的最佳解釋。選項 C 內容亦與文章不符，無須考慮；選項 B 與 D 乃表示會增加輻射物質的檢測，並無法構成安全的理由；以選項 A 所述最適當，故選 A。

答案	題目中譯	解題攻略
5. **(B)**	從這封信與文章，我們可以得到甚麼結論？ (A) 台灣無法避開輻射毒害的影響。 **(B) 不需對日本核能外洩感到恐慌。** (C) 日本的食物發現有危險的輻射物質。 (D) 商業與人權國際研討會將會延期，直到核能危機結束。	此題要選可由郵件及文章得到的結論。除了選項 B 之外，其他選項內容皆與內文不符，故選 B。

📝 長文閱讀 14

中譯

　　嗨，琳達，很高興見到妳！我是潔西卡，人事部的人事專員。我來跟妳介紹妳主要的工作項目。妳將在我們辦公室裡扮演非常重要的角色。舉凡辦公室的雜務，像是接聽電話、招募新人、安排旅遊、信件服務、傳真、影印、掃描、文件歸檔、處理敏感的人事文件以及跑腿，妳要負責非常多的事。想要表現稱職，妳必須監督負責招待的志工、在董事會與委員會議作會議記錄、為所需文件做文書處理。此外，擔任接待工作也是妳的職責，招呼訪客並將其轉介給適當的部門成員。妳要維持大廳跟櫃台區的乾淨與整潔。既然妳已經有相關的工作經驗，妳應該知道公司期望妳協助職員處理行政事務，並完成其它指派的工作。最後但同樣重要的，妳要負責訂購辦公室用品並監控存貨。好吧，大概就這樣子。妳下午會領到妳的員工證。希望妳在這裡工作愉快。

答案	題目中譯	解題攻略
1. **(A)**	根據這篇談話，琳達擔任那一項工作職位？ **(A) 辦公室助理。** (B) 人事專員。 (C) 軟體工程師。 (D) 行政主管。	本題在問 Linda 所負責的工作職務為何。由文章所述，可知選項中應以「辦公室助理」最符合其所描述之工作職務內容，故選 A。
2. **(B)**	下列何者不屬於琳達的職責範圍？ (A) 幫忙員工們處理必要的行政事務。 **(B) 維持廁所與餐室的清潔。** (C) 將客人交給合適的部門之前，先接待一下客人。 (D) 招募新人和跑腿。	本題要選出 Linda 職責範圍外之工作。由文章所述可知 Linda 的工作範圍並不包括「維持洗手間和茶水間清潔」，故選 B。
3. **(C)**	我們從這篇談話中可以知道？ (A) 琳達之前沒有工作經驗。 (B) 琳達正在面試一個工作。 **(C) 琳達今天第一天上班。** (D) 琳達將跟潔西卡在同一個部門工作。	本題要選讀者可由此文推論之事。由文章主旨在向 Linda 介紹工作內容，並在結尾告知 Linda 今天會領到工作證，可知今天應為 Linda 第一天到職上班，故選 C。

答案	題目中譯	解題攻略
4. **(B)**	這篇談話目的為何？ (A) 應徵新員工。 **(B) 介紹Linda的主要的工作項目。** (C) 介紹一個新進人員。 (D) 討論提案。	由談話中提到：Let me introduce you the main tasks of your job.（我來跟妳介紹妳主要的工作項目。），故推知答案為 B。
5. **(C)**	根據這篇談話，下列選項何者為真？ (A) Linda不必接聽電話。 (B) Jessica是Linda鄰居。 **(C) 如果LInda想要表現稱職，必須監督負責招待的志工。** (D) 維持大廳跟櫃台區的乾淨與整潔不是Linda的職責。	由這篇談話中中間部分提到：To fill the position capably, you have to provide supervision to reception volunteers...（想要表現稱職，妳必須監督負責招待的志工），故推知答案為 C。

中譯

Bon Appetit 法國餐廳暫停營業通知

　　東京皇家花園管理部證實，日本公平貿易委員於九月十日對本飯店的Bon Appetit餐廳菜單上某些品項涉嫌產地不實展開調查。

　　飯店管理部相當嚴肅地看待此事，已決定讓Bon Appetit餐廳在得到進一步通知前暫停營業。

　　指控中具體地舉出Bon Appetite菜單中前澤菲力牛肉被替換為山形菲力牛肉這個例子。

　　飯店的管理團隊目前針對此事正進行調查並將與地方當局全力配合。

　　皇家花園為此事對貴客們所造成的不便深感抱歉，且已採取一連串措施以確保此類事件不再發生。

2011年九月十二日
Benjamin W. Bowie
總經理
東京皇家花園

答案	題目中譯	解題攻略
1. **(D)**	這份公告想要傳達什麼訊息給顧客？ (A) Bon Appetite 菜單上的前澤菲力牛肉將改為山形菲力牛肉。 (B) 日本公平貿易委員會將在東京皇家花園舉辦記者招待會。 (C) Bon Appetite 餐廳將停止營業做整修。 **(D) Bon Appetite 餐廳被控以不同產地的材料取代菜單上一些菜色。**	本題在問此告示想傳達何種訊息給顧客。選項 A、B 與 C 所述之內容皆與告示內容不符。故以選項 D 最為適當。
2. **(D)**	根據這份公告，飯店如何處理這個狀況？ (A) 他們想要採取法律訴訟來反駁這個不實的指控。 (B) 他們計畫召開記者會來說明整個來龍去脈。 (C) 他們承諾會嚴厲地處罰這些怠忽職守的人。 **(D) 他們讓餐廳暫停營業並針對此事展開調查。**	本題在問飯店對此情況的處理方式。由告示內容可知飯店暫停了餐廳的營運，並將深入調查此事，故選 D。

答案	題目中譯	解題攻略
3. **(B)**	我們從這份公告可以做何推論？ (A) Bon Appetite 菜單上的菲力牛肉完全是由美國進口。 **(B) Bon Appetite 餐廳將停止營業一段時間。** (C) 東京皇家花園一定會應付地方當局。 (D) Bon Appetite 餐廳被勒令停止營業以殺雞儆猴。	本題在問讀者可由告示推論之事。由告示內容可知餐廳將暫停營運一段時間，故選 B。
4. **(A)**	根據這份公告，misrepresentation的意義與下列那一個字最接近？ **(A) 謠傳。** (B) 目的。 (C) 決定。 (D) 描述。	misrepresentation意思為不實陳述或誤傳，故推知答案為 A。

答案	題目中譯	解題攻略
5. **(D)**	根據這份公告，下列何者為真？ (A) 指控中具體地舉出 Bon Appetite 菜單中山形菲力牛肉被替換為前澤菲力牛肉這個例子。 (B) Bon Appetit 法國餐廳在九月十號重新營業。 (C) 日本公平貿易委員於八月底對本飯店的 Bon Appetit 餐廳菜單上某些品項涉嫌產地不實展開調查。 **(D) Bon Appetit 法國餐廳將暫停營業。**	由公告提到，為配合調查，將暫停營業，故推知答案為 D。

📝 長文閱讀 16

中譯

　　不管你將它稱之為分期付款協議、支付協議、付款方式或付款計畫，其實都是同一個意思－繳付所欠稅款。聽起來似乎不錯，但一次付清全額稅金其實可以為你將你所須支付的利息與罰款減至最少。然而，對於無法馬上清償欠稅的人而言，分期付款成為一個較可以接受的付款方式。分期付款可以將稅金以較小額、較易處理的方式繳付。

想要透過分期付款協議來繳稅的納稅人，若積欠：

- 小於等於一萬五千美元的合併稅、罰款以及利息，可以利用線上繳款協議（OPA）或撥打帳單或通知書上的電話號碼。可線上索取的分期付款協議申請表A1表格（PDF），可寄到您帳單上的地址。

注意：如果您最近已送交所得稅申報表及稅款，卻未收到帳單，可以利用線上付款協議來設定今年度申報的分期付款協議。

- 大於一萬五千美元的合併稅、罰款以及利息，仍適用此分期付款協議，但是需填好B3（PDF）表格的個人資料收集聲明。撥打帳單上面的電話或者將分期付款協議申請，包括A1（PDF）和B3（PDF）表格寄到帳單上的地址。

會以書面通知告知您的分期付款協議是否被核准或者需要修改。

解析

答案	題目中譯	解題攻略
1. **(C)**	這則資訊主要是關於什麼？ (A) 如何要回多繳的稅。 (B) 哪裡可以下載A1表格。 **(C) 如何分期付稅。** (D) 到哪裡繳交A1和B3表格。	這題在問主旨。由文意可知此篇文章主要在討論以分期方式繳付稅款，故選C。

答案	題目中譯	解題攻略
2. **(A)**	下列何人最有可能需要這些資訊？ **(A) 無法立即清償稅款的人。** (B) 迴避罰款與利息的人。 (C) 想在商業銀行開個儲蓄帳戶的人。 (D) 想要在網路填寫申報個人稅申報表的人。	這題在問最有可能需要此資訊的人。由文章內容在討論分期繳稅，可知需要此資訊的人應為無法立刻一次繳清稅款的人，故選 A。
3. **(B)**	寄出分期付款協議申請給相關單位後，在甚麼情況下可能會收到書面通知？ (A) 三個月內未繳款。 **(B) 當分期付款協議申請通過時。** (C) 當未繳兩期帳款時。 (D) 如果簽了一筆十二個月分期，但又想改成六個月付完。	這題是問在何種情況下，申請分期付款合約的人會收到紙本通知。由文章內容可知在合約核准的情況下會收到紙本通知，故選 B。

答案	題目中譯	解題攻略
4. **(D)**	根據這份資訊，penalties 意義違和？ (A) 個人。 (B) 薪資。 (C) 原則。 **(D) 懲罰，罰金。**	penalties是指罰款，如果不確定，可由：but you can save money by paying the full amount you owe to minimize the interest and penalties you'll be charged....（但一次付清全額稅金其實可以為你將你所須支付的利息與罰款減至最少）推知和金錢有關，故推知答案為 D。
5. **(B)**	如果您最近已送交所得稅申報表及稅款，卻未收到帳單，你可以如何處理？ (A) 可忽略。 **(B) 你可以利用線上付款協議來設定今年度申報的分期付款協議。** (C) 致電銀行處理。 (D) 文中並未提及。	由Note提到：: If you recently filed your income tax return and owe but have NOT yet received a bill, you can use the Online Payment Agreement to establish an installment agreement on current year returns.，故推知答案為 B。

📝 長文閱讀 17

中譯

親愛的金恩斯太太，

我六週前有寫信給你，要求退給我那筆買了瑕疵麵包機的款項。我已將麵包機退回，而你們的退貨部門也寫信通知我已收到退貨。從收到那封信到現在已經三週了。除了我已如購買合約上所說的退回了你們的產品，卻還沒收到收到換貨或是退款。

我對你們公司已經非常有耐心了，但我現在不要換貨，因為我急著要用麵包機，所以已經買了一台。所以可否請你們盡快把錢退回給我？ 我已經給你們回應我要求的時間，相信你能了解我的立場。

我將你們公司退貨部寄給我的信件影本寄給你，希望能對你們盡快退錢給我有所幫助。我相信你們也會退回我將產品寄回你們公司所花的運費新台幣兩百元。

非常感謝您對此事的關注並期待你迅速的回應。

潔思敏·羅倫絲謹上

解析

答案	題目中譯	解題攻略
1. **(C)**	這封信件的主要目的為何？ (A) 解釋麵包機送貨延誤的原因。 (B) 通知家電零售商貨物有一部分損壞。 **(C) 要求退回瑕疵麵包機的款項。** (D) 要求換一台麵包機。	由信件內容可知信件主旨在要求瑕疵麵包機的退款。故選 C。

答案	題目中譯	解題攻略
2. **(A)**	根據這封信，潔思敏羅倫斯目前為止從退貨部那邊收到了些甚麼？ **(A) 一封告知他們已收到瑕疵品的信。** (B) 一筆包含麵包機的退款以及運費的錢。 (C) 更換在運送期間損壞的物品。 (D) 購買協議和發票。	這題在問 Jasmine Lawrence 目前為止從退貨部門得到什麼。由信件內容可知她只收到一封通知已收到瑕疵產品的信件。故選 A。
3. **(B)**	根據這封信，以下敘述何者為誤？ (A) 潔思敏羅倫絲已經買了另一台麵包機。 **(B) 潔思敏羅倫絲想換另一台麵包機。** (C) 潔思敏羅倫絲依照購買合約將產品運還給公司。 (D) 潔思敏羅倫絲認為公司應負擔運費。	這題要選出錯誤的敘述。依信件內容可知 Jasmine Lawrence 並不想再拿到替換的產品，故選 B。
4. **(A)**	根據這封信，第一段出現的單字defective與下列何字意義相近？ **(A) 有瑕疵的。** (B) 專業的。 (C) 完美的。 (D) 流利的。	由將麵包機退貨，可以推知此機器可能有些問題或毛病，故推知答案為 A。

答案	題目中譯	解題攻略
5. **(C)**	關於Jasmine敘述，下列何者為真？ (A) 她接受麵包機換貨。 (B) 她上週寫信給金恩斯太太。 **(C) 她急著要用麵包機，所以已經買了一台。** (D) 她寄回公司所花的運費新台幣一百元	(A) 錯誤，她要退款。 (B) 錯誤，六週前。 (C) 正確。 (D) 錯誤，是兩百元。 故得知答案為 C。

長文閱讀 18

中譯

> 親愛的吳珊卓小姐，
>
> 　　很高興告訴你，你已經成功地度過三個月的試用期且管理單位一致決議要聘用你為先鋒出版社的長期員工。
>
> 　　鑒於你令人滿意的表現，你已確定擔任先鋒出版社執行編輯一職且你的薪水已調整為新台幣三萬三千元，自2011年七月一日起生效。每月最晚五號可領到薪水。
>
> 　　如果你有任何疑慮或問題，請與你的主管討論。
>
> 茱蒂巴倫
> 管理部長
> 2011年六月十日。

❸
長文閱讀測驗—中譯&解析

答案	題目中譯	解題攻略
1. **(A)**	這封信的主要意旨為何？ **(A) 通知收件人她已被正式聘用。** (B) 通知收件人她將被轉到其他部門。 (C) 通知收件人她的工作表現令人不滿意。 (D) 跟收件人解釋她被開除\的原因。	由內容可知此信主旨在通知收件人她已通過試用期，被正式錄用。故選A。
2. **(B)**	吳珊卓小姐何時起將正式成為先鋒出版社的正式員工？ (A) 從2011年六月十日起。 **(B) 從2011年七月一日起。** (C) 由本信發出日期起計 (D) 跟她的主管討論之後。	此題在問 Sandra Wu 何時將正式成為正式員工。由信中with effect from 07/01/2011（自2011年7月1日起）可知答案為 B。
3. **(D)**	下列何者在信中未提及？ (A) 吳珊卓上班的地方。 (B) 吳珊卓在這家公司做了多久。 (C) 吳珊卓的月薪。 **(D) 吳珊卓主管的名字。**	此題要選出信中未提及之事。由內容可知除了Sandra主管的名字之外，其他選項的內容都有出現在信件中。故選 D。

答案	題目中譯	解題攻略
4. **(C)**	這封信的最佳標題為何？ (A) 短期雇用公告 (B) 迎新派對通知 **(C) 長期員工雇用郵件** (D) 新公司廣告	由信中提到：We are pleased to convey that you have successfully completed three months of probation period ...（很高興告訴你，你已經成功地度過三個月的試用期），故推知答案為 C。
5. **(D)**	根據這封信，下列何者為真？ (A) 人力資源部經理撰寫此信。 (B) Judy是出版社執行編輯。 (C) Sandra的薪水已調整超過新台幣三萬五千元。 **(D) Judy對Sandra表現滿意。**	由信中提到：In view of your satisfactory performance, you have been confirmed at the position of Executive Editor...（鑒於妳令人滿意的表現，你已確定擔任執行編輯一職），故推知答案為 D。

📝 長文閱讀 19

中譯

親愛的顧客，

遺憾地，八月一日起我們必須調漲衛生紙／面紙的售價。
新的售價為：
衛生紙　十二包 新台幣一百五十元
面紙　　五十包 新台幣九十九元

很抱歉我們必須做這樣的調漲，但是這樣子我們才能繼續
為我們的顧客提供高品值的衛生紙／面紙。也就是説我們將持
續供應令顧客感到物超所值的商品。
我們感激您的光顧且期望未來繼續為您服務。

誠摯地，

Lynn Farmer
星星超市經理

解析

答案	題目中譯	解題攻略
1. **(D)**	從這份公告我們可以知道？ (A) 這裡將舉辦清倉拍賣。 (B) 紙巾沒有庫存了。 (C) 商店不接受網路訂購。 **(D) 商店將調高紙巾的售價。**	此題要選出可從此公告中得知之事。由公告表示衛生紙價格將有所調漲，可知應選D。

答案	題目中譯	解題攻略
2. **(B)**	這份公告想向顧客傳達什麼訊息？ (A) 週年慶特賣將從八月一日開始。 **(B) 某些商品八月一日起將漲價。** (C) 八月一日起商店將關閉一個月。 (D) 商店八月一日起將停止供應衛生紙／面紙。	此題要選公告欲傳達給顧客的訊息。此公告旨在通知顧客店內特定產品價格調漲，故答案為 B。
3. **(A)**	下列何者在公告中未提及？ **(A) 漲價的原因。** (B) 漲價的項目。 (C) 漲價生效日。 (D) 店經理的名字。	此題要選出公告內未提及之事。由內容可知公告雖知會顧客漲價一事，卻未說明漲價的理由。故選 A。
4. **(A)**	根據這份公告，competitive這個單字 最接近下列何者選項？ **(A) 價格較好。** (B) 昂貴的。 (C) 消極的。 (D) 奢華的。	由offer high quality products with competitive prices（供應令顧客感到物超所值的商品），表示價格比較有競爭性的，故推知答案為 A。

答案	題目中譯	解題攻略
5. **(B)**	這份公告的最佳標題為何？ (A) 新超市促銷 **(B) 價格調漲通知** (C) 大清倉廣告 (D) 新產品網路銷售	公告裡提到衛生紙和面紙調漲，故推知答案為 B。

📝 長文閱讀 20

中譯

Hello Sunday's ® 對自己好一點

開胃菜買一送一

　　不得轉售。限在Hello Sunday's ®餐廳的店內用餐才有效。遺失或失竊不再補發。一次消費一桌限使用一張折價券。不得與其他優惠共用。不含稅金與小費。除非法律規定，否則單據不能退換現金或用來支付小費。有效期限到2011年12月31日。只在台灣有效。折扣限用於等價或較低價的餐點。© 2011 Hello Sunday's Inc.

　　折價券編號： HSENTREE30669

　　效期： 01/12/11-31/12/11

答案	題目中譯	解題攻略
1. **(A)**	優惠券何時生效？ (A) **2011年十二月起。** (B) 2011年十二月一日止。 (C) 2011年十二月三十一日起。 (D) 沒提到。	這題在問優惠券何時生效。由優惠券上的有效期間為01/12/11-31/12/11可知從2011年的十二月就開始。故選 A。
2. **(B)**	下列敘述何者為非？ (A) 優惠券限用於台灣的 Hello Sunday 餐廳。 (B) **客人出示優惠券可享有外帶主菜免費。** (C) 優惠券無法跟其他的優惠活動合併使用。 (D) 優惠券持有人就算不想去 Hello Sunday's 用餐也不能將它賣掉。	這題要選出錯誤的敘述。由優惠券上 for dine-in-only（只限內用），可知這張優惠券無法使用於外帶餐點。故選 B。in combination with 表示「與…合併使用」；preferential activity 為「優惠活動」之意。
3. **(C)**	如果優惠券掉了或失竊，客人能怎麼辦？ (A) 出示證件以要求換發。 (B) 向餐廳要求賠償。 (C) **只能接受事實。** (D) 在拍賣網站上另買一張。	這題在問優惠券遺失或遭竊時該怎麼辦。由優惠券上表示此券不得轉售以及不得補發，可知一旦遺失或遭竊只能自認倒楣，故選 C。

答案	題目中譯	解題攻略
4. **(D)**	Hello Sunday's 是哪種商店？ (A) 藥局。 (B) 雜貨店。 (C) 超市。 **(D) 餐廳。**	由開胃菜和第一句提到是餐廳，故推知答案為 D。
5. **(D)**	Neil預定一桌四人，請問他可以用多少張折價券？ (A) 4張。 (B) 3張。 (C) 2張。 **(D) 1張。**	由第二行提到：One coupon, per table, per visit. （一次消費一桌限使用一張折價券。不得與其他優惠共用。），故推知答案為 D。

📝 長文閱讀 21

中譯

親愛的張湯姆先生，

　　我們一直都希望在這段公司的艱難時期，我們可以將所有員工都留在公司。不幸地，事情未能如我們所願。

　　因此，很抱歉，我們必須通知你2011年六月三十日之後你將無法繼續在此服務。我們非常滿意你在雇用期間所展現出來的才能，也對於失去這樣一位公司員工感到很可惜。

　　請接受我們對你未來最高的祝福。

人事部經理

解析

答案	題目中譯	解題攻略
1. **(D)**	這封信的主要目的為？ (A) 為他們犯錯所造成的不便道歉。 (B) 向張湯姆的升職道賀。 (C) 提供張湯姆轉職到他們公司的機會。 **(D) 通知張湯姆他已被解除職務。**	此題在問信件的主旨。由信件第二段的 unable to utilize your services（無法繼續聘用）可知此為一封解雇通知信，故選 D。
2. **(A)**	根據這封信，公司何時將終止對湯姆的雇用？ **(A) 2011年七月一日起。** (B) 2011年六月三十日起。 (C) 一個月後。 (D) 沒提到。	此題在問公司停止任用的時間。由信件內容可知在 June 30, 2011之後停止，意即隔天，也就是7月1日，故選A。
3. **(A)**	在信中的第二段，utilize的意義與下列那一個字最接近？ **(A) 運用。** (B) 補給。 (C) 拒絕。 (D) 退回。	utilize 與 apply 皆有「運用」之意，故選 A。

答案	題目中譯	解題攻略
4. **(B)**	人事部經理為何炒張湯姆魷魚？ (A) 他不滿意湯姆的表現。 **(B) 公司面臨艱難時期。** (C) 湯姆最近工作都遲到。 (D) 他常常和湯姆爭執。	由信件第一段提到：We had been hoping that during this difficult period of reorganization we could keep all of our employees with the company.（我們一直都希望在這段公司的艱難時期，我們可以將所有員工都留在公司。），故推知答案為 B。
5. **(C)**	根據這封信，下列何者為真？ (A) 所有員工都會丟掉工作。 (B) 湯姆收到信後就將無法繼續在公司服務。 **(C) 主管非常滿意湯姆在雇用期間所展現出才能。** (D)湯姆決定離職。	由第二段：We have been pleased with the qualities you have exhibited during your tenure of employment with us...，故推知答案為 C。

中譯

供給種類	停止期間	影響地區/建物	停止原因
淨水	2011年三月二十五日晚上十點（星期五）到2011年三月二十六日早上六點（星期六）	台北市－停水將影響大安區到信義區的一些營業場所	進行水管改造工程

請注意上面列出的區域將暫停供水。抱歉造成不便。

請注意供水可能會比預計早一點恢復，也有可能會碰到意料之外的狀況或事件而需要延長停水。如果需要進一步的資訊，請撥打我們的二十四小時顧客服務熱線 0800-345-678。

解析

答案	題目中譯	解題攻略
1. **(A)**	這個通知的主要用意為？ **(A) 宣布停水。** (B) 申請失業救濟金。 (C) 拒絕出席會議。 (D) 限電通知。	這題要選公告主旨。由公告內容可知此為一停水通知，故選 A。
2. **(C)**	水要停多久？ (A) 24小時。 (B) 18小時。 **(C) 8小時。** (D) 36小時。	這題要選停水時間。由公告上表示停水時間為 3/25 晚上十點至 3/26 上午六點可知停水將歷時約八小時，故選C。

答案	題目中譯	解題攻略
3. **(B)**	根據這個通知，停水的原因為？ (A) 執行水質檢測。 **(B) 執行水管改造工程。** (C) 落實節約用水政策。 (D) 懲罰用戶未繳交水費。	這題要選停止供水的原因。表格中有明文表示是：Alteration work on water mains to be carried out（進行水管改造工程），故選 B。片語 put… into effect 表示「落實……」之意。
4. **(C)**	下列那一種狀況是通知中沒提到的？ (A) 可能會提前恢復供水。 (B) 停水可能因無法預見的狀況而延長。 **(C) 名單所提及之外的地區可能會無預警受停水影響。** (D) 顧客服務熱線是提供給需要進一步資訊的民眾。	這題要選出公告中未提及的狀況。除了選項 C 之外，其他三種狀況都可在公告中看到，故選 C。
5. **(B)**	如果需要任何進一步資訊，你該如何呢？ (A) 傳真到顧客服務。 **(B) 撥打我們顧客服務熱線。** (C) 上網查詢答案。 (D) 打手機號碼洽詢。	由倒數第二行提到：Please call 0800-345-678, our 24-hour Customer Service Hotline, for further information. 故得知答案為 B。

中譯

親愛的先生，

　　我叫林布萊恩，我想要在你們飯店訂一間房，含食宿住三晚。

　　我太太跟我會在 2011 年一月十五日禮拜六約下午四點抵達。2011 年一月十八日禮拜二早上十點離開。

　　我們想要一間湖景雙人房。如果沒有雙人房，雙床的房也可以。

　　請給我們離娛樂設施遠一點的房間且房內要可以上網。

　　下列是我的聯絡資訊。
　　手機號碼： 0912-345-678
　　傳真號碼： 076663888

林布萊恩

親愛的林先生，

　　這封信是您在假日度假酒店訂房的確認函。您的確認碼為 6088。確認您將待三個晚上，從 2011 年一月十五日到一月十八日，雙人床的房間一間。一晚台幣五千六百元。很抱歉，目前沒有湖景房。

　　這是預定保證函，需在您抵達的二十四小時前取消訂房才能退款。謝謝您選擇我們的飯店。我們期盼您的光臨。

假日度假酒店 謹上

解析

答案	題目中譯	解題攻略
1. **(B)**	林布萊恩的信主要目的為何？ (A) 取消訂房。 **(B) 訂房。** (C) 約會延期。 (D) 回應邀請。	本題要選出 Brian Lin 信件的主旨。由信件內文可知此乃一封訂房信，故選 B。
2. **(C)**	下列何者不是林布萊恩在信上指定的特別需求？ (A) 想要住在遠離娛樂設施的房間。 (B) 想要住在可以上網的房間。 **(C) 想要住在有市景的雙人房。** (D) 想要住在全天供餐的飯店。	本題要選出何者非 Brian 信件中提出的特殊要求。由信件內容可知 Brian 要求的是一間湖景房，而非市景房，故選 C。full board 指「包含全食宿」，也就是除提供客房外，另提供所有餐飲。
3. **(B)**	布萊恩跟他太太預計何時離開飯店？ (A) 約一月十五日下午四點。 **(B) 一月十八日中午前。** (C) 一月十八日下午。 (D) 一月十五日早上十一點之後。	此題在問 Brian 夫婦何時離開飯店。由 Departure … on January 18, 2011, … at ten. 可知他們將在1月18日中午前離開。故選 B。

答案	題目中譯	解題攻略
4. **(C)**	從確認信中我們可以做何推論？ (A) 飯店不提供上網服務。 (B) 飯店不提供早餐。 **(C) 所有湖景房都被訂光了。** (D) 飯店不接受取消訂房。	此題要選出可由確認信函推論之事。由 no rooms available with a lake view （無空的湖景房）可知湖景房已被訂滿，故選 C。
5. **(B)**	如果布萊恩想取消訂房並退款，最晚何時須跟飯店聯絡？ (A) 抵達的兩天前。 **(B) 抵達的一天前。** (C) 抵達的半天前。 (D) 抵達的兩小時前。	此題在問 Brian 若要退房並可拿回退款，必須最晚何時通知飯店。由確認信中表示 must cancel at least 24 hours before ... （必須最遲於 24 小時之前……）可知應選 B。

中譯

親愛的莊先生，

B&R公司很高興提供您技術協調員的工作機會。我們相信您的知識，技術和經驗將會是我們最具價值的資產之一。

如果您接受這個工作機會，基於公司規定您自受聘日起將可享有下列待遇。

- **薪資：** 年薪分月支付直接入帳。
- **績效獎金：** 最多可達年薪的百分之三，分季入帳。
- **福利：** 標準福利，B&R提供給支薪員工的福利包含
- 三節禮金
- 勞保與健保
- 享病假，婚假，產假，等等。
- 享特休與事假

這封信有附一份聘用契約。請在到職日當天簽署之前先詳細閱讀。

最好的問候，
B&R 人力資源管理部

聘用契約

將 B&R Co. Ltd. 稱為「公司」，而莊麥克斯稱為「員工」。

公司聘用員工且員工在此同意於下列事項與條件下接受聘雇：

1. 職責：員工同意執行本文件所載的職責：
- 研究電腦操作系統相關資訊
- 檢討目前的操作系統，做系統變更甚或研發操作系統
- 與顧客，專案經理以及其他公司員工保持聯繫
- 行政職務
- 準備每天例行工作的報告，圖，表以及評估結果。
- 擔任此項職務的員工除了平常習慣的職務外，須更進一步於公司所從事的其他相同或相似的事務上執行職務。

2. 報酬：綜上所述，公司每年將就員工的服務支付員工新台幣九十一萬元的薪水。

3. 聘雇期間：2011年七月一日起，員工契約持續生效直至其中一方終止契約。

4. 終止：下列情況下契約可能提前終止（1）員工死亡或生病或喪失工作能力以致一年內超過三週無法執行職務且（2）員工違反契約。由雇主做決定並以掛號信發出通知，由雇主送到員工的地址。有了這份通知，契約將停止且於寄出通知的七天後完全結束。

5. 雜項：（1）員工同意得聘雇期間或其後不得洩露公司的交易資訊。（2）契約中如有任何爭議，應依循中華民國仲裁協會的規定進行有約束力的仲裁以議決。

雙方於2011年七月一日起於B&R Co. Ltd.執行此合約，特立此證。

公司

＿＿＿＿＿＿＿＿＿＿＿＿＿＿＿＿＿＿＿＿＿

員工

＿＿＿＿＿＿＿＿＿＿＿＿＿＿＿＿＿＿＿＿＿

答案	題目中譯	解題攻略
1. **(A)**	從信與文件中我們可以知道？ **(A) B&R 提供莊麥克斯工作機會。** (B) B&R 從莊麥克斯現任職的公司將他挖角。 (C) B&R 向莊麥克斯道賀升職。 (D) B&R 邀請莊麥克斯留任。	此題要問讀者可由以上信件及文件得知何事。依信件開頭表示 offer you a job（提供您一個工作）以及文件標題為 employment agreement（任用合約）可知 B&R 正提供對方一個工作機會。
2. **(B)**	根據這份契約，下列何者不是B&R 技術協調員的職務？ (A) 研究電腦操作系統相關資訊。 **(B) 導入區域技術計劃。** (C) 與顧客聯繫。 (D) 準備每天例行工作的報告。	本題要考不在合約中所列技術協調員的職務範圍之內的工作內容。依內容可知選項 B 所述並非其工作職責，故選 B。

答案	題目中譯	解題攻略
3. **(A)**	根據這份契約，在何種情況下 B&R 將終止對莊麥克斯的聘雇？ **(A) 莊麥克斯因病超過三週無法工作。** (B) 莊麥克斯請一週的病假。 (C) 莊麥克斯工作第一天就請婚假。 (D) 莊麥克斯沒有按時領到薪水。	這題問在何種情況下 B&R 將停止聘用 Max Chuang。由合約內容可知選項 A 為正解。
4. **(C)**	人力資源處在信中沒有提到那一項福利？ (A) 年終獎金。 (B) 婚假。 **(C) 喪假。** (D) 健康保險。	本題要選出哪項福利並未在人資管理部給 Max Chuang的信中被提及。依信件內容所列之福利並未提到 funeral leave（喪假）可知此題應選C。
5. **(D)**	公司多久支付莊麥克斯薪資一次？ (A) 三個月一次。 (B) 隔週一次。 (C) 一週一次。 **(D) 一個月一次。**	這題在問公司將多久支付Max Chuang 薪資一次。由信中說明 annual … salary paid in monthly installments …（年薪按月支付）可知薪資支付一月一次，故選 D。

中譯

瓊的服裝店訂購單

傳真訂購專線：993-660-2211

數量	品名	型號	尺寸	顏色	單價
2	上衣	TP3066557	6	米白	190
1	裙子	SK2255369	6.5	棕	390
1	短褲	SO1002538	6.5	黑	290
1	泳裝	SW0033501	S	粉紅	480

	小計：	1540
☐ 普通包裹 – 新台幣80元	運費：	120
☑ 快遞 – 新台幣120元		
總價：		1660

聯繫人姓名	艾曼達蕭
電話號碼	978-363-5400
聯繫人地址	17 Prospect St. W. Newbury, Mass 01985
送貨地址	同上
電子信箱	Amanda1013_hsiao@gmail.com
付款方式	☐ 萬事達付費 或 Visa
	信用卡號碼
	☐☐☐☐ ☐☐☐☐ ☐☐☐☐ ☐☐☐☐
	有效日期
	☐☐☐☐☐☐
	d d m m y y
	☐ 銀行轉帳
	☑ 貨到付現
訂貨日	2011/4/21

收信人：艾曼達蕭小姐
寄件人：瓊的服裝店
主旨：訂單 #10667

親愛的蕭小姐，

　　非常感謝您訂購我們的產品。很抱歉，必須跟您說部分您四月二十一日（訂單 #10667）訂單內所要的物品目前無庫存。我們的供應商說這些東西最快下個月底也就是五月三十一日才會到貨。缺貨項目如下所列：

　　　　裙子一件　　　尺寸 6.5 棕色
　　　　泳裝一件　　　尺寸 S　粉紅色

　　如果您因無法馬上拿到產品而想要取消上面的任何一項物品，請告訴我們，否則，當它們一到貨，我們就會將您訂購的產品以隔天到貨的方式快遞寄出。您最遲於六月一日就可以收到。至於您訂購的其他項目，我們今天下午五點前會寄出，明天中午就會到達您的送貨地址。

　　請接受我們對所有可能對您造成的不便誠摯的歉意。

瓊的服裝店
謹上

答案	題目中譯	解題攻略
1. **(C)**	這則廣告的目的為何？ (A) 通知客戶信用卡已無法使用。 (B) 通知客戶訂單已取消。 **(C) 通知客戶部分訂單商品缺貨。** (D) 通知客戶不久之後店家將停止營業。	這題在問郵件的主要目的。依郵件內容可知這是封通知顧客部分訂單缺貨的信件，故選 C。
2. **(A)**	顧客的訂單想要怎麼付款？ **(A) 現金。** (B) 信用卡。 (C) 分期付款。 (D) 貸款。	這題在問顧客要如何付款。由訂貨單上顧客勾選「貨到付款」，可知顧客將以現金付費，故選 A。
3. **(B)**	在甚麼情況下，蕭小姐應該盡快跟瓊的服裝店聯絡？ (A) 如果她想要取消全部的訂單。 **(B) 如果她想要取消目前沒貨的項目。** (C) 如果她沒辦法用信用卡付款。 (D) 如果她的物品在運送過程中有損傷。	這題在問在何種情況下蕭小姐應盡速聯絡店家。根據郵件內容可知若她想取消缺貨品項則應盡速聯絡店家，故選 B。

答案	題目中譯	解題攻略
4. **(A)**	顧客收到第一批貨時需要付多少錢？ **(A) 新台幣七百九十元。** (B) 新台幣一千五百四十元。 (C) 新台幣一千六百六十元。 (D) 新台幣八百七十元。	這題在問顧客收到第一批貨品時應支付的貨款。根據訂貨單上的報價，可知應為台幣 790 元，故選 A。
5. **(A)**	下列資訊何者未在上面的表格與郵件中提及？ **(A) 服裝店的位置。** (B) 顧客的連絡電話。 (C) 店的傳真訂購號碼。 (D) 顧客下單的日期。	這題在問未在以上訂購單及電子郵件中提及之資訊。由信件及訂購單上皆未出現服飾店的地址，可知答案應為 A。

中譯

親愛的員工們，

我們很高興地宣布為了慶祝大家去年宜人的表現，我們將在2011年三月三十一日舉辦公司旅遊。這個公司旅遊不只是為了慶祝公司最近的擴展，也是為了獎勵所有員工辛勤的工作，讓公司得以成為業界頂尖的服務提供者。

我們鼓勵大家帶家人一起參加，因為公司旅遊同時也是公司家庭的旅遊。一整天都有競賽，摸彩，以及其他的活動。為了確認出席狀況，請跟安娜或者活動規劃部的任何成員聯繫或者直接回覆這封信。

安娜克拉克森
活動規劃部

親愛的安娜，

謝謝你關於公司旅遊的通知函。我很高興有這麼一個好機會能跟其他小組和部門的人聚聚，這樣也可以擴大朋友圈。可以帶我的家人參加公司旅遊也是個好消息。我只是想知道是否有參加人數的限制。如果沒有的話，我想帶我家裡所有成員一起去，也就是我父母，我太太，我的兩個小孩，我弟弟跟弟妹以及他們的三個小孩。如果我不能把他們全部帶去，請盡早讓我知道。

感謝你迅速的回覆。

傑克哈里森
研發部編輯專員

答案	題目中譯	解題攻略
1. **(B)**	傑克哈里森的信目的為何？ (A) 通知活動規劃部他無法參加公司旅遊。 **(B) 詢問公司旅遊每個員工參加人數的限制。** (C) 要求公司旅遊的活動安排細節。 (D) 推薦一個公司旅遊的好地方給活動規畫部。	這題在問 Jack Harrison 所寫信件的主要目的。由信件中可知他想知道參加公司旅遊是否有人數限制，可知答案為 B。
2. **(C)**	下列資訊何者未在通知函中提及？ (A) 公司旅遊的目的。 (B) 公司旅遊的舉辦日期。 **(C) 公司旅遊舉辦的地點。** (D) 公司旅遊的負責部門。	這題要選通知信中未提供之資訊。由信中並未提及公司旅遊的地點，可知答案應為C。
3. **(A)**	傑克哈里森希望安娜克拉克森在回信中跟他說甚麼？ **(A) 參加人數是否有限制。** (B) 是否須負擔任何活動的費用。 (C) 公司旅遊要辦多久。 (D) 如果無法去公司旅遊，他是否需要請假？	這題在問 Jack Harrison 希望對方在回信中告知之事。由信件內容可知他想知道是否有參加人數限制，故以 A 為正解。

答案	題目中譯	解題攻略
4. **(A)**	傑克哈里森想帶多少人跟他一起去公司旅遊？ (A) **十個。** (B) 九個。 (C) 十一個。 (D) 沒提到。	這題在問 Jack Harrison 打算帶多少人一起參加公司旅遊。由信件內容計算人數，可得到答案為10人，故選A。
5. **(C)**	我們可以從上面的郵件中推論出？ (A) 公司旅遊一年辦一次。 (B) 公司去年的業績不令人滿意。 (C) **公司最近可能剛開了分公司。** (D) 公司想要裁掉一半員工。	這題在問可從以上郵件中推論之事。由信件內容可知公司近期內有擴充規模，推測選項 C 應為正解。

語研力 E080

英文閱讀高分特訓：
克漏字＋解題攻略，閱讀力及成績倍速飆升

作　　者	黃琪惠
顧　　問	曾文旭
出版總監	陳逸祺、耿文國
主　　編	陳蕙芳
執行編輯	翁芯琍
美術編輯	李依靜
法律顧問	北辰著作權事務所

印　　製	世和印製企業有限公司
初　　版	2023 年 04 月
出　　版	凱信企業集團 - 凱信企業管理顧問有限公司
電　　話	（02）2773-6566
傳　　真	（02）2778-1033
地　　址	106 台北市大安區忠孝東路四段 218 之 4 號 12 樓
信　　箱	kaihsinbooks@gmail.com

定　　價	新台幣 360 元 / 港幣 120 元
產品內容	1 書

總 經 銷	采舍國際有限公司
地　　址	235 新北市中和區中山路二段 366 巷 10 號 3 樓
電　　話	（02）8245-8786
傳　　真	（02）8245-8718

國家圖書館出版品預行編目資料

英文閱讀高分特訓：克漏字＋解題攻略，閱讀力及
成績倍速飆升／黃琪惠著. -- 初版. -- 臺北市：凱信
企業集團凱信企業管理顧問有限公司, 2023.04
　面；　公分
ISBN 978-626-7097-73-1(平裝)

1.CST: 英語 2.CST: 讀本

805.18　　　　　　　　　　　　112001848

凱信企管

用對的方法充實自己，
讓人生變得更美好！

凱信企管

用對的方法充實自己，
讓人生變得更美好！

凱信企管

**用對的方法充實自己，
讓人生變得更美好！**

凱信企管

用對的方法充實自己，
讓人生變得更美好！